Herman Mayer

An American patriotic drama, in four acts: entitled The Patriots: or, Scenes and incidents of the revolution

Herman Mayer

An American patriotic drama, in four acts: entitled The Patriots: or, Scenes and incidents of the revolution

ISBN/EAN: 9783337306359

Printed in Europe, USA, Canada, Australia, Japan

Cover: Foto ©Andreas Hilbeck / pixelio.de

More available books at **www.hansebooks.com**

AN AMERICAN PATRIOTIC DRAMA,

IN FOUR ACTS:

ENTITLED

THE PATRIOTS

OR

Scenes and Incidents of the Revolution.

ARRANGED BY

HERMAN MAYER,

FOR THE

Centennial Anniversary

OF

American Independence,

A. D. 1876.

With Cast of Characters, Stage Business, Costumes, Relative Positions, &c., &c.

MASSILLON, OHIO:
S. & J. J. HOOVER, PRINTERS.
1876.

THE PATRIOTS.

DRAMATIS PERSONAE.

General Washington.   General Conway.
General Greene.   Colonel Frazier,
Benjamin Franklin.   John Hancock.
Thomas Jefferson.   John Adams.
Samuel Adams.   Joseph Warren.
Richard Henry Lee.   Charles Carroll.
Stephen Hopkins.   Clerk of Congress.
1st Congressman.   3rd Congressman.
2d Congressman.   4th Congressman.

Bellman of State House, Philadelphia.
Buell Pomeroy, a Patriotic American.
Doctor Lincoln, a Physician from Boston.
Captain Preston, a British Officer.
Seth Peabody, a Live Yankee.
Crist O'Reilly, a Patriotic Irishman.
Jacob Krout, a Patriotic Dutchman.
Sampson Foster, a Patriotic Negro from Old Wirginny.
Curry, ⎫ Tories.   Otis, a Whig.
Stuart, ⎭   Soldier.
Rose Creighton, Betrothed to Buell.
Kate Creighton, Betrothed to Doctor Lincoln.
Two Boys, Two Girls, Two Ladies' Maids, Servant, Twelve Continental Soldiers, Orderly, Five Riders of the Santee, Ten British Soldiers, Congressmen, Citizens and Goddess of Liberty.

N. B.—Sixteen Males and Four Females will fill speaking characters.

THE PATRIOTS.—COSTUMES.

Washington; First Dress, General's uniform, Second, Stuart's Picture.

Gen. Greene, Gen. Conway, Col. Frazier and Richard Henry Lee; Continental General's uniform.

Jefferson, John Adams, Hancock, Franklin, Warren, Clerk of Congress, Carroll; Citizen's Dress 1776, black.

Hopkins; Quaker garb and hat, drab.

Samuel Adams; A red suit cut of 1776.

Congressmen; Continental suits cut of 1776.

Bellman, An old man's suit.

Buell; First Dress, Blue overshirt and belt, kneebreeches; Second, Riders of Santee Dress; Third, Major's uniform.

Doctor Lincoln; First Dress, Surgeon's uniform; Second, Citizen's suit, rich black.

Preston; British uniform, scarlet trimmed with white facings.

Seth; First Dress, Knee-breeches, old fashioned coat, red waist-coat, long Yankee hair; Second, Continental Captain's Uniform.

Krout; Dutch suit; Second, Hunter's uniform.

Crist; Irish Suit; Continental Soldiers uniform.

Sampson; Negro Suit; Officer's old coat.

Curry and Stuart; Cutaway coat & kneebreeches.

Otis and Citizens; Same.

Rose and Kate; First Dress, costumes of 1776; Second, Wedding Suits.

Girls and Maids; costumes of 1776.

Continental Soldiers; Blue coats with buff facings, three corner hats, white breeches, black belts.

British Soldiers; Red coats and faced with blue, white breeches, high boots, white belts, high hats.

THE PATRIOTS.

ACT I.

Scene i — *Interior of House in Boston in 1775, 4 G. Window in Flat. L. H. practical.* John Hancock, Samuel Adams, John Adams *and* Joseph Warren. *seated at table in C.*

Han. Pursuant to instructions from the Boston Town-Meeting held yesterday at Faneuil Hall, we have met and prepared *this* last appeal of our colony to his Majesty King George III for redress of all its grievances and its protest against the presence of the troops in our city, which is now ready for our signatures. If this petition is laid aside, unnoticed and treated with contempt, as all have been, then we must look for redress to the proposed Union of all the Colonies and declare our rights, and, declaring them, maintain them. (*Signs*)

S. Adams. We must have our rights, and now is the time to strike a home blow, or we may as well sit down under the yoke of tyranny. There is no room for delay! We want a Union of Colonies! If the Colonies do not now unite, they may bid farewell to liberty, burn their charters, and make the best of thraldom. (*Signs.*)

J. Adams. I fear all hopes for a reconciliation are in vain. While we have prayed for personal security and liberty, the right of property, the power of local legislation, and waited for a gracious answer to our petitions from the King, we were invaded by an armed force, im-

pressing and imprisoning the persons of fellow-country
men, contrary to an express act of Parliament   To con-
tend against our parent state is, in my idea, the most
shocking and dreadful extremity; but tamely to relin-
quish the only security we and our posterity retain for
enjoyment of our lives and properties without one struggle, is so humiliating and base, that we cannot support
the reflection.   (Signs, and remains sitting during next
speech.)

S Adams It is a direful extremity, yet it is lawful to
resist the chief magistrate if the commonwealth can not
otherwise be preserved.   The time has come when we are
called on to defend our liberties and privileges.   I hope
and believe we shall, one and all, resist even unto blood,
yet I pray God Almighty that this may never so happen.

Warren. (*Signs.*) What wonder that we feel roused to
stern and nervous resistance?   Boston to-day looks like
a town in a state of siege.   The guns of the ships in our
harbor are pointed on the town, troops are ashore with
muskets charged, bayonets fixed, and a train of artillery
marching through the streets of Boston ; Boston Common, Faneuil Hall, all public places and buildings are filled
with soldiers ; sentinels stationed in the streets, and people challenged as they pass to and from church.   Are not
our liberties gone when an army is billeted on us in time
of peace ?   Our fellow-countrymen dare not meet in public and deliberate on grievances, unless troops are at once
dispatched to disperse the meeting.

Han. The presence of the military in Boston is a per-
petual source of irritation and excitement, and it is hardly
possible but that a collision far more shocking than the
Boston Massacre, or the Custom House Riot as some call
it, must soon take place.   The soldiers look on the people
as turbulent, factious, and needing discipline : the people
regard the soldiers as instruments of tyranny and outrage.
Mutual insults and provocation will result.

S. Adams. The troops must be removed, and we are appointed to wait upon the Governor and the Royal Commander to have them removed at once, or a fearful collision will be certain to ensue.

Warren. Yes, the colonists are making plans for effectual resistance, and are preparing for any case of emergency. They are continuing to secure arms and military stores secretly, and are organizing to be prepared to assert their rights when time and circumstances should give to their claim the surest prospect of success.

J. Adams The New England Militia alone, when once under command of their old and experienced leaders, such as Putnam, Stark and Ward, will be a formidable host against the few regiments of British Regulars that are in our midst. Other Colonies will not let us sacrifice ourselves alone for our common cause; they will muster as many troops as New England, headed by officers of equal experience, and by their united efforts we will resist the obnoxious measures of the British Ministry which they are trying to enforce on us by the troops. An appeal to arms and the God of Battles is all that is left us.

Han Our colony means to resist; we have witnessed very bold and decided steps which the people of Boston took at their late meeting in regard to the high-handed measures of the government, and they are well aware that their action must bring them into direct collision with the mother country. But their spirit is roused; if blood *must* be shed, the colonists are ready for even that last and searching appeal.

(CURRY AND STEWART, *two tories, appear at window on the outside and listen.*)

S. Adams The colonists are determined on Independence; yet they know the blood and treasure independence will cost. They will never think of it 'till *driven* to it as the last fatal resort against ministerial oppression, which will make the wisest mad and the weakest strong.

Han We are driven to it; history does not furnish an instance of revolt begun by the people which did not take its rise from oppression. And what people have been oppressed more than the people of America, and particularly of those of New England? Should it come to a resort to arms, Almighty God himself will look down upon our righteous contest with approbation. We will be a band of brothers, strengthened with inconceivable supplies of force and constancy by that sympathetic order which animates good men, confederated in a good cause.

It seems we are assigned by Divine Providence in the appointed order of things, the protector of unborn ages, whose fate depends upon our virtue.

J. Adams. America seems summoned to play a great part in the history of the world. I always consider the settlement of this country with reverence and wonder, as the opening of a grand scene and design in Providence for the illumination of the ignorant, and the emancipation of the slavish part of mankind all over the earth

Warren. The adjourned meeting called to convene at Faneuil Hall will call for an American Congress, which should come together in New York, and to consist of committees from each of the Thirteen Colonies, to be appointed respectively by the delegates of the people, without regard to the other branches of the Legislature, and devise a plan for a Union.

S Adams. That is a step in the right direction. The colonies have many statesmen and orators, men great in action, from which the delegates can select to represent their respective colonies, and whose influence once exerted, will bring matters to an issue. A Congress, and then an Assembly of States, is no longer a mere fiction in the mind of the political enthusiast.

Han. And in that Congress imagine Virginia, that rang the alarm bell of Independence for the Continent, represented by that champion of Independence, Patrick Henry; Edmund Pendleton, its graceful and persuasive speaker; that logician Richard Bland; that witty George Wythe; the noble hearted Peyton Randolph; the scholarly Richard Henry Lee, commonly styled the Virginia Cicero; the young Col. Washington, who espouses the cause of his country; and last, but not least, among the many able sons of proud Virginia, the young philosopher and patriot, Thomas Jefferson.

Warren. South Carolina can send from among many bold and able champions of their country's rights, John Rutledge, who some account the rival of Patrick Henry; the intrepid Christopher Gadsden; the enlightened politician Henry Laurens; Edward Rutlege & David Ramsay.

J. Adams. Other southern colonies have such distinguished patriots as Wm Hooper, Thomas Lynch, Jr.

Button Guinett and Lyman Hall. Pennsylvania has Benj. Franklin. Robert Morris, George Clymer and George Ross New York has the Livingtons, Lewis Morris, Wm. Floyd and others.

Warren. Let us not forget that New England could lend assistance in council by Josiah Bartlett, Eldridge Gerry, Stephen Hopkins, Roger Sherman, Oliver Walcott. Why, Massachusetts alone can be represented by a host of popular leaders and champions of liberty, in no others than Thomas Cushing, James Bowdoin, Josiah Quincy, Robert Treat Pain, not forgetting my illustrious fellow committeemen, John Hancock, John Adams, and our fire-brand, Samuel Adams, the *Original Incendiary* of this revolution, who King George wants transported to England. Put the destiny of America into the hands of such a Congress, supported by our brave colonists, who have fought England's wars against the savages and French for 100 years, without any assistance from their mother-country, and they will build a union that will reach from Florida to the icy plains of Canada! and drive tyranny from these northern climes!

S. Adams. We have enlisted in the cause of our country, and are resolved at all adventures to promote its welfare. If the colonies are accomplishing a revolution for the emancipation of mankind, there is no fitter moment than this: the sound of war everywhere else on the earth has died away. Kings will sit still in awe, and nations turn to watch the issue.

Warren. Gentlemen, we have performed our charge; now let us retire to meet our countrymen at Faneuil Hall, and there make known our deliberations. Exeunt. R. 2 e.

SCENE II.—*A Street in Boston.* 2 G. *Stage dark. En-ter* CAPTAIN PRESTON *and* CURRY, *L.* 2 *E., go to C.*

Pres. Well, Curry, you were successful then in watching those self-styled [*sneeringly*] patriots. They have about run to the end of their rope. I was certain that they, above all others, know the intention of the Colonists. because they are acknowledged leaders.

Curry. Yes, Captain Preston, I chanced to overhear some very important information concerning the movements of the Colonists, who are all rebels against the Home Government (CRIST *appears at Wing, R*) But we must hasten to inform the Governor of that meeting they are going to have at Faneuil Hall, and spoil that for them.

Crist. (*At Wing, shaking stick at them,*) Arrah, ye rascals! yees intind to inform the Governor, do yees? I wonder what they mean. Faith, I think I'll keep my eyes on yees.

Pres. We must have the whole batch of them kidnapped and transported to England for trial.

Crist (*At Wing*) Yees are to kidnap somebody. Oh, ho!

Curry. Captain, is there not a standing reward of £1000 for the apprehension of either Samuel Adams, John Adams, Hancock, and some more of them?

Christ. (*At Wing*) Saml. Adams. John Adams and Hancock, is it? I think I'll get the whole of the secret after a while.

Pres Yes, there is £1000 offered as a reward by the King for each of them, if brought to England for trial They are rank rebels and the cause of all this trouble

Crist (*At Wing*) A thousand pound for each, is it?

Curry. Couldn't we manage to get them aboard of a sloop in the harbor, with a little assistance from your soldiers? Once aboard they are safe, and our fortune is made.

Crist (*At Wing*) By my soul; faith, I don't think yees 'ill make that fortune, not while my name is Crist O'Reiley.

Pres. Curry, we will decide on this hereafter. At present we must lose no time to check the movements of the Colonists I shall continue you in his majesty's service as a spy. Go, and keep your eyes on those great rebels, the patriots, and I shall report to the Governor of our discoveries Meet me at Faneiul Hall at their meeet ing. (CURRY *exit at R.* PREST. *going to L meditating.* CRIST *comes down.*)

Crist (*Shaking stick at* CURRY) Oh, you dirty, thieving rascal. I'll go wid you, and keep my eyes on you, and them patriots, too, ye may dipind on it. I think I'll continue meself as a spy in the service of the Boston boys— I have it, I'll go down and tell the boys of this, and if they or anybody else attempts to lay hands on them blessed saints, Adamses and Johnny Hancock, at the meeting, mind ye, there'll be such a spilling about of English and Tory brains one would think you had no need of them in your lousey skulls. (*Follows Curry off.*)

Prest (C) Another meeting. Then there will be more shedding of blood. When sage advisors and grey headed veterans revolt, desperate must be the resistance of the young generation. If the Colonists are all of the same metal that made up the mob in the late riot down at the Custom House, England will have her hands full in bringing them to submission. All is not well. (*Placing his hand on his heart*). I have a strange feeling within me, that bodes no good. Besides smarting under the sharp lashes of that firebrand Saml. Adams, and that terrible oath of vengeance made by that Buell, the leader of the ruffians; one chiding me for my too hasty action in dispersing the mob by force of arms, the other cursing me and swearing vengeance on my head for the untimely death of the boy Willie Creighton, who fell amongst the rioters. I'm the prescribed victim of their wrath. The thought is horrible! 'twill drive me mad. (*Walking to R. and L.*) There is one consolation left me: As an officer in His Majesty's service, and commander of the forces doing duty in the city, I obeyed the instructions of my superiors and did my duty. (*Boldly on R*) These rebels must be taught to respect the government. (*Looking L*) Ah, who comes here?

Enter Seth, L , *with papers.*

Seth (*aside*). Consarn my skin, if there ain't that blood thirsty captain that came nigh butchering the whole of us the other day; I guess I'll turn back, he may sorter mistrust I had a hand in that mess.

Prest. Well, sir, what is your business out this time of night?

Seth. Wall, I thought as how a fellow might walk the streets at night and 'tend to his business, without being molested; you see its kinder dangerous to be out at day, no telling what these regulars would do. I've some papers for the Governor.

Pres O, dispatch, I perceive.

Seth. Yes, I conclude they are something of that sort. (*Peeping into them.*)

Pres. Prying knave, give me the papers (*Snatching at them.*)

Seth. Oh, no you don't! You see they are not directed to you; they are for the Governor, and, as it kinder happins that I am the postmaster, I reckon it's my duty to deliver 'em into the right hands

Pres. Yes, so it seems.

Seth Yas, the governor will 'tend to these, and I guess the people would be a little better satisfied if his excellency would attend to them and all his other affairs.

Pres You do! And pray what are the people's designs? Do they intend to resist the measures taken by the ministry?

Seth Why, a rat will resist if you pen him.

Pres. And do the people consider themselves penned? (*Seth looking sternly at him*)

Seth. Why, that's a matter of opinion; it's pretty much as folks think nowadays. But seeing that the troops hold the town, and the people hold the country, (which cuts off your supplies), its a matter of doubt who are the worst penned.

Pres And if the people had possession of the town. what would they presume to do?

Seth Why, now that's rather hard to say; but seeing that they made a bon fire of the stamps, and a big tea pot of Boston Harbor, it's but nat'ral to conclude they would do pretty much as they damn please!

Pres. Indeed! And are they aware that such things will bring down chastisements on their rebellious heads?

Seth Why, they kinder calculate on a little disturbance.

Pres. Thou immovable pest! And do you call an open rebellion nothing more than a disturbance? I suppose, if the truth were known, you are among the rest of the *loyal* subjects who object to his majesty's troops occupying a small part of the town

Seth. Why, the people have come to a conclusion that

their assistance is not wanted, as we calculate to do all our own fighting.

Pres. And pray who gave the people *liberty* to come to any such conclusions without the sanction of his majesty's authorities?

Seth. Liberty? hem! (*Aside.*) As I'm a chap he's looking for, I reckon it's best not to say too much.

Pres Thou cautious knave! I believe thou art as great a rebel as the worst of them; and if the truth were known you were a participant in the Custom House Riot.

Seth. (*Aside*) I thought so I must be bold. Take care what you say; it's agin the law to call a man a rebel unless you can prove it.

Pres. Talk to me of the law! Go on about your business, and don't loiter about the streets! If I find you on my return I shall arrest you. (*Exit L*)

Seth Wall, I reckon I know my business; of course, I'd went if he would have been right sot on it, but seeing as how the fool let me have my own time about it, I'll take my time.

Enter Sampson, L., Sneaking along.

Wall, I do declare, if that nigger ain't afraid of his shadow. (*Slapping him on shoulder.*) See here, Mister, where are you trying to creep to.?

Samp. (*On his knees.*) Spar me! Spar me!—O, Lord! O, Lord!—Oh, is dat you, Massa Sef?—Ha, ha, ha! (*Rises*) I thought it was one of those pestered Britishers. You know they don't like us colored persons. I am so skirred anyhow at night. Daytime I don't fear man, debel, Britisher nor anybody else.

Seth. Wall, where are you steering for, anyhow?

Samp. You see, Massa Sef, it's getting mighty hot for niggers here in Boston, and case I was at that row de oder day, where my colored brudder Attucks was killed, I'se gwine to make tracks for the hills whar de rest of the boys are learning soldjering. I declare I'se bound to give them Red coats a blow for revenge, somehow, Squire Sef.

Seth. You seem to be somehow familiar with my name. I can't recollect of having any introduction to you.

Samp. I doesn't, neader, but my name's Sampson. I seed you down wid de crowds after the skirmish the odder day, whar good old Massa Adams larruped dat British Ossifer so awfully wid his tongue, for shooting down the people and killing dat little Willie Creighton arter he got down on his knees and begged the soldiers to spare his life. Don't you remember me, Squire Set?

Seth. Yas, I kinder remember you now, but consarn me, I can't remember whar I heard that name before—kinder familiar, too. Sampson—Sampson—Sampson—Let's see—

Samp. Dat's it, Sampson—Ha, ha, ha; you know. Sampson, dats it. Sampson, what slewed the Phillistines!

Seth Sure enough! Sampson did slay the Phillistines—

Samp. Dats de name. dats it. Ha, ha, ha—

Seth. Slew ten thousand of them with the jaw-bone of an ass.

Samp. Dats my name; he slewed ten thousand asses wid a jaw-bone—Ha, ha, ha!—Golly!—was you thar? Sampson, dats my name, dats me.

Seth. Is it? Wall, you are just the chap I want. That ar' same British officer insulted me just afore I seen you, and he has about ten thousand asses under his command, who think they can run the town, and now I want you to go down and slew everyone of them 'afore breakfast.

Samp. I kin do it, Massa Sef, slew every cussed one of them, if I gets a right square butt at 'em, but you must wait till sun-up.

Seth. Why wait till morning?

Samp. Why, you see, I is so dam scared at night.

Seth. Well, all right, screw up your courage to the sticking point for the morning. Come on. (*Exeunt L.*)

SCENE III.—4, G. *A public ground in the vicinity of Bos-ton. Enter* BOYS *and* GIRLS *all talking, and in great excitement. R. and L.*

1st Boy. Have you heard the news?
2d Boy. Yes, but is it true?
Sally I haven't, what is it?

Sarah. Yes, what is it?   (*Confusion.*)

1st Boy. There has been a great battle between the Americans and British out at Bunker Hill, bigger than Lexington and Concord put together.

2d Boy. No, no, you've got it all wrong; it was Breed's Hill.

1st Boy. I say it was Bunker Hill.

2d Boy. And I say it was Breed's Hill.

Enter SAMPSON, *L. 1 E.*

Samp. Bunkum! Bunkum! I know all about it.

1st Boy. There! I told you so.

Samp. I seed de man what brought de Post Office; he's coming here pretty soon, and he'll give you the whole discourse.

2d Boy. Well, *I* heard it was Breed's Hill.

Samp. Doesn't I tell you it was Bunkum?

Enter KROUT. *R.*

Krout. Preed's! Preed's Hill! I knows me all about das.

Samp. What? what? why I jest seed the man wid de letter-bags; he's bin to de camp and brought de news and he said it was Bunkum

Krout. Yaw! yaw! he got bunkum! Abber Dunder and Blitzen, I knows me all about it, and I dell you it vas on Preed's Hill—Preed's.

Enter SETH, L.

Seth. Bunker, Bunker, or there's no snakes in Connecticut.

Krout. I say it was Preed's Hill, and the Yankees got licked.

Seth. What, if you say that agin, I'll jump down your throat and stop digestion for o month.

Samp. It's lucky you is a white man—if you was a nigger I'd butt your head off

Seth. He ain't no white man, neither, he's a Dutchman.

Krout Yam, but I'm a Pennsylvania Dutchman, and I'll fight for das country till I was melted away.

Seth. Then you'll last all through the war, for it would take several July suns to thaw you

Samp. Here comes de Post Office.

(*Enter* BUELL, *R. All crowd round him, ask questions in rapid succession.*)

Seth. Well, Captain, where was it?

Samp. Who got licked?

Krout. Was it Preeds or Bunker?

Samp. How many got wounded?

Buell. Give me a little breathing time; I cant answer you all at once.

Seth. Silence, you inquisitive varmints! Now go it. What's the news?

Buell. There has been another battle fought by the Americans and British; and tho' we lost possession of the fortifications, the enemy were twice repulsed with fearful slaughter.

Omnes. Hurrah! (*Confusion.*)

Buell. We have every reason to be satisfied with the result. But our little army needs more men

Seth. Boys, I'm going in—will you jine me? We'll enlist, and follow old Putnam.

Omnes. Aye, Aye, hurrah! hurrah!

Seth. I ain't much given to speech-making, but on this occasion, I am wound up to such a pitch that if I don't speak I'll bust.

Omnes. Speech! Speech!

Seth. Hem! Gentlemen and Krout:—

Krout. Dat vas me.

Seth. It is with feelings of the liveliest indignation and delight that I address you. I make a motion and second it—that a regular volunteer regiment be raised out of the inhabitants of this city, (*Shout*) for a more enlightened and unsophisticated population cannot be found anywhere around; they are distinguished for their wisdom and their bravery, present company excepted. (*Shout*) The tea trade of England, I am told, has been considerably weakened by the large quantity of water with which it was mixed in Boston Harbor. (*Shout*) Fellow citizens and Sam :—

Samp. And dat's me.

Seth. In raising this company, I will, with your permission, elect the officers. I therefore nominate Jacob Krout as the First Lieutenant of the company, because he can play the fife; Sampson, as Second Lieutenant, to march behind and carry the target. Shout for the nominations. (*Omnes shout.*)

Krout. I decline de nominations! I aint a dutch musician, and I won't blow my brains out, and my wind out for nobody.

Seth. (*Seeing Buell going*) Don't go, Captain, until you see us organize—

Buell. Certainly, sir, I'll see you organize, although I have some important packages from General Putnam to deliver, and must be off shortly.

Samp. And I begs leave most disrespectfully to recline the target. I ain't gwan to be put down to de foot ob de class.

Seth We unanimously refuse to accept the resignations —and if I find any discontended volunteer guilty of subordination, I shall treat them with quiet contempt, and hang them accordingly. (*Shout.*) Come along, prepare to muster men, (*Going.*)

Krout. Stop! stop a little! Who's de Captain?

Seth. I forgot him; we will put it to vote. All those in favor of my being Captain, will signify by saying "Aye."

Omnes. Aye!

Seth. All those to the contrary, shut up. (*Pause*) Elected unanimously, by Gosh! (*Shouts.*)

Krout. So, so, dot was the Yankee way to make a Captain. (*All going*) Stop a little, mine friends from Roxbury and Cambridge was coming to enlist.

Seth. We want more recruits, and seeing as how we have to wait a little, and have an old soldier with us, I propose that he tell us something about his army experience and make us feel brave. (*Girls going.*) Hold on, girls Now liven us up with a story.

Samp Yes, massa, the story of Braddock's war.

Krout. Yaw, yaw; I like me dot story. My fader fighted in dot war.

Omnes Did he?

Krout. Oh, yaw, he drove a paggage wagon. (*Omnes laugh*)

Seth Fire away—I'm all ears.

Sally. I always told you that, Seth. (*Omnes, Ha,ha,ha.*)

Buell. Well, folks, sit down; you shall have my story
We started out, two thousand strong, with General Braddock, stiff and firm as a poker, at our head, and among
his aids was a young Virginia Colonel, a fine, tall, com
manding officer, who rode his horse like a king, and looked
like an emperor born, from hat to heel. The sun shone
on the scarlet dresses of the Regulars, and the green and
blue coats of the Provincials We were advancing gaily
through the woods, when we beheld a long, lean fellow of
a hunter, with a slouching hat covering his features, a
rough coat of skins covering his back, and a rifle on his
shoulder. We saw this strange looking hunter talking to
the commander and his staff, and presently information
ran along the line that this individual had been engaged
to lead the troops to Fort Du Quesne. On we went, and
red coat and green frock were all emerging from the wood,
when there came a scene that would have made your
blood run cold. Sudden as lightning, there flashed from
every bush around us the fire of a concealed enemy. This
guide betrayed us I could see one red-coat officer after
another fall to the ground, while near me my comrades
fell, wounded and dying, at every shot; and in the thick
est of it all, with his manly form towering above the
smoke of battle, was the young Virginia Colonel—George
Washington—his form a target for every French musket
ball! (*Omnes Sigh*)

Seth. Whar is that Colonel now?

Buell. I venture my life he is in the ranks with his
countrymen, and he'll make a great General some day.

Crist. (*Outside*) Hurrah for Washington. (*Enter L*)
Hurrah for Washington! hurrah! (*All rise*) Oh, my
darling Buell, your young Virginia Colonel has been appointed the big General-in Chief of the Continental Army
of the Continental Congress, and he is now on way
up to Boston. Hurrah! hurrah!

Omnes. (*Wild shouting.*)

Buell. Then our country is safe!

Seth. Fall in! I now dismiss this com   o go
home, and all of you go home and kiss your d   s and
mammies, and sweethearts good bye, and if y   ve no

sweetheart of your own, kiss somebody else's, but be sure and assemble here promptly at a minute's notice. (*They rush for the girls, who run off R. and L, and all follow.*)

Enter WASHINGTON *and* COL. FRAZIER. *L S. E.*

Fra. General, 'twould be an idle form to congratulate you upon your accession to the command of the American Army; it has been the urgent wish of your countrymen, and we, your associates, honor the day on which they made so wise a choice.

Wash. Nay, sir, you honor me too much; if my heart has swelled with pride at the flattering preferences that Congress has seen fit to show towards me, with what gratitude do I hear that those with whom I have been so long associated approve of its choice.

(*Enter a Sergeant, L 2. E.*)

Ser. A courier has arrived in haste, and desires an interview with the Commander-in-Chief.

Wash. Bid him enter. (*Enter Buell, L. 2 E.*)

Wash. Welcome, young friend, your business with me?

Buell. I have in my possession a dispatch, which I was enjoined to place in the hands of the Commander-in-Chief by Genl. Putnam. (*Gives dispatch to* WASH.)

Wash. Excuse me Colonel. (*Retires up stage.*)

Buell. Why, Colonel Frazier, have you taken the field again. I thought your long service in Braddock's War had tamed the fire in your blood (*Shakes hands.*)

Fra. Buell, is that you. I am glad to see you. Yes, I have taken the field again. To be candid with you, I thought, too, my blood was tamed, but you know the effect of martial music on the ears of a veteran. The first sound of the rattling drum and squeaking fife sent the blood tingling to my finger ends; they itched 'till they grasped a sword; they itched, sir, they itched, and here I am.

Buell. Ha! ha! I would have supposed your snug homestead and plantation on the Delaware would have proved more attractive than camp life.

Fra. My homestead—'twould give me poor shelter; it has been burned to the ground, and I, ha! ha! ha! I have been obliged to burrow in the earth like a rabbit.

Buell. Your house burned by the British?

Fra. No, sir, by worse men, bad Americans—Torie
Give me a true-hearted Englishman for an enemy, and I'll
shake hands with him and fight him in the same breath.
But a Tory, a traitor to his country—ah, sir, an honest
man don't know how to meet those fellows.

Buell. 'Tis true, I much prefer an open enemy.

Fra. On our way thither we heard rumor of a battle at
Bunker Hill. Came you direct from the front?

Buell There was a terrible battle at Bunker Hill. I
came from Boston Neck, where the Americans bivouacked
after the battle. The dispatches I bore may possibly re-
late to the affair.

Wash. (*Advances*) Gentlemen, I have here received a
dispatch from Genl. Putnam; a battle has been fought at
Bunker's Hill. (*All turn eagerly to* WASHINGTON.) Generals Howe, Piggot and Clinton commanded the English
forces

Fra. All of them accomplished soldiers and vigorous
men, a formidable host to cope with.

Wash. (*Reading.*) "Our forces had fortified the hill,
and waited with cool and steady purpose the approach of
the enemy; on, on they came; they halt, and then a death-
like pause ensued." (*To* FRAZIER) Read, sir, read!

Fra. (*Reading*) "In the next moment, the fire of the
British opened upon us; they advanced till the whites of
their eyes was visible At that instant a sheet of flame
glanced from our lines like lightning in a cloud, while, at
one report, a thousand of our muskets were added to the
uproar."

Wash. Oh! what a scene of blood and carnage. Our
freedom will be dearly purchased—many a desolate hearth
will mourn the day. Proceed, sir.

Fra. (*Reading*) "As the smoky veil was lifted and
sailed heavily away, a fearful scene opened to our view.
The hill was strewn with dead and dying, the British
troops were flying from the hill; they soon rallied, and
came on in treble numbers; our ammunition was exhaust-
ed, and we retired, covering our retreat with clubbed mus
kets and sinewy arms " (*Hands paper to* WASHINGTON.)
It seems then that the English gained the hill, but with
fearful loss.

Buell. One more such victory would be a death-blow to England's cause.

Wash. (*Who has been reading*) Generous, noble-hearted Putnam! he gives to Prescott the honor of the day, and with his proverbial modesty claims no share of praise.

Fra 'Tis his nature to be self-sacrificing. With such men to embrace our cause, we have but little to fear. (*Regarding* WASHINGTON *reading*) But see, the General's moved

Buell His face, that just betokened joy, seems shadowed now by sorrow.

Fra. Speak, General; what ill tidings have you read? We have shared your joy, let us partake your grief.

Wash Ill tidings, indeed, the gallant young Warren has fallen in the action (*Pause*) Well may it cast a gloom upon us *He has fought to the death* in defense of his rights. (*All uncover*) In the requiem over those who have fallen in this action, time with his eternal lips, shall sing the praise of Warren. Colonel, we must secure a true and tried soldier, to undertake a hazardous journey south, with instructions to the different commanders, concerning the movements of their armies, such as we may this day determine by a council of war.

Fra General, fortune favors us in no less a person than our young countryman here, who was instructed even with the dispatches just read. If I may be permitted I would suggest to your excellency, to intrust this man with an independent command, say, of one hundred men, mounted for special service—each bearing in his bosom a heart swelling with patriotic fire like his, and he will lead them, in spite of all British, where our country needs their service.

Wash. Then, accompany me, and I will commission you instantly; if deeds of daring and danger be your aim, you shall not long pine for opportunity. Come! (*All exeunt L. 2 E.*)

Music—Yankee Doodle.

Enter—SETH, °SAMPSON, KROUT *and 6 boys, with guns, pitchforks and miscellaneous military accoutrements.*

Seth Halt! Front face!—'Tention company! Dress!
—Krout, put in your corporation!

Krout (*Drawing himself in*) Dere, dat ish de pest
vat I kin do!

Seth. (*Looking behind the line*) Oh, consarn your picture, that's jest as bad as the other side Come out of
the ranks! Now, take a fair and impartial view of the
regiment! What d'ye think of that for a turn out?

Krout Splendit!

Seth. Now, as you are Leftenant of the reg'ment, make
'em a sharp speech, and immortalize yerself.

Krout. Vel, if I breaks town, you must help me out!
Hem! Shentlemen, of das Kaiserrech :—

Samp. Aye, golly, we'se a gwine to have a sour krout
oration!

Seth. Silence in the ranks!

Krout. I ish a billin' over mit grandure and patriotism!
Der enemy of our country is landed on our shores, and
every man wat ish a man, must do his duty like a man,
or he don't vas a man at all.

Omnes. Hurrah!

Krout. Frien's, countrymen, unt I may say—frien's—
dey must be driven pack on ter pint ov der pagnet, und
my advice is, dat you fight as bad as never vas pehind or
pefore!

Omnes. Hurrah!

Krout. I've got some little pizness to tend to mineself,
but just so soon as ter vight is over, I vill be dam! Believe me!

Omnes. Hurrah!

Krout. So, up mit ter panner! traw your muskets, und
shtrike for freedom! (*Hits* SAMPSON *on stomach with
flat of sword.*)

Samp. Look'ye heah! look'ye heah! Who you hittin'?

Seth. Silence, in the ranks! If the honorable gentleman
from Africa don't restrain his feelings, I'll have him
whitewashed immediately.

Samp. Golly! nigger will be nigger, if you whitewash
him all ober.

Seth. 'Tention, the hull! Shoulder, arms!

Samp. Why, Massa Sef, we is a sojering arms!

Seth Well, then, you ain't disobeying orders. Now, Order arms! (*They order arms very irregularly*) That's right—there's nothing like precision in military tactics. Shoulder arms, again! Present, arms! Charge, bagnets! (*They all make a rush at* SETH, *who is in front*) Hold on, halt! stop! you tarnal critters, do you want to kill the Captain? As you were! Shoulder arms, again! Order arms, again! Draw, ramrods! Return, ramrods! (SAMP-SON *walks to extreme end of the line, and gives his ramrod to a soldier.*)

Seth. Now, then, what on airth are you a doin'?

Samp. Didn't you say return ramrods? I borrowed dat from Massa Jake.

Seth. Well, then, it's all right. 'Tention, the hull! Screw up your courage! The enemy's in front of you, and glory's behind you; let each man feel as strong as Julius Cæsar, with the jawbone of an ass. Forward, march! (*Music—Yankee Doodle. Exeunt.*)

Quick Drop—and raises on Tableau, "Washington Crossing the Delaware."

ACT II.

SCENE I.—*Front of State House, Philadelphia. Open Belfry on State House. Bell in sight. Door* C. *of* F. *Enter* OTIS *and* CURRY, L , *talking* CITIZENS, BOYS, &C., *enter opposite side*

Otis I tell you, sir, this is a momentous day in the deliberations of the Continetnal Congress.

Carry. And I tell you this day will pass as have the past twenty days, in debating the subject, then they will adjourn to meet and debate again.

Otis. To-day Congress will adopt a declaration declaring our country free from the crown of England. We are no longer to be tyrannized over by King George the Third and his oppressive laws. To-day our country—do you hear the words—our country will be declared free and

independent.   I had these very words from Sam Adams'
lips.

Curry   Free and independent! [*Laughs.*] It will not
be worth the talk that's been made over it.   George the
Third is not so easily deprived of his rights over the
Colonies.   Let Sir Henry Clinton or Lord Howe get hold
of John Hancock, Sam Adams, Mr. General Lee, or any
of this Continental Congress, or Mr. General Washington
or any of those Generals, and we will see the greatest
hanging since the days of hold Tyburn in Hengland.

Enter BUELL *followed by* CITIZENS, *1st* L *entrance* BUELL
leans on his rifle and listens

Stuart.   You kin talk it, you kin, as our old nigger
Pompey ses; and your sentiments is mine; cause why,
the Continental Congress wants to set niggers' free too.
I'd sooner be a subject of any George, or Jim, or Jeff,
thin to see niggers set free, I would.

Otis.   Well, you are two "pretty" creatures, you are,
for freedom!—You—

Buell.   Talk it plain, Mr. Otis; talk it plain.

Otis.   [*To* CURRY,] You infernal tory, you love oppres-
ion—[*To* STUART] and you are a cowboy and traitor
Such as you are unfit for freedom as a rattlesnake would
be to play with children   A tory and a cowboy!

Curry.   I am a born Hinglish subject, and a Hinglishman is a Hinglishman forever.   You are a whig, and want
to ruin the country.   Let any of his majesty's officers get
hold of you!

Otis.   Get hold of me?   If they do, it will be with a
musket in my hands, fighting for the Colonies.   Mr. Englishman, if you like to live in America, submit to the will
of the majority.   The stores are all closed in Philadelphia
to-day, and the people are anxiously waiting for the announcement of the Declaration.   This fourth day of July,
1776, will be a famous one in history.

Curry.   Famous for the mark it will make for the hang-
man; I would'nt close a shop of mine for no day like this
If I'm a tory, there's thousands more like me in this
country.

Stuart.   Yes, and plenty of cowboys like me; and us
tories and cowboys will cause you whigs—

Buell. To give you more Lexingtons, Concords, and Bunker Hills. [*To* CURRY] You're an Englishman, that's some excuse for you; you don't know any better. (*To* STUART) But you're American born. Why, you are one of the vilest of the vile on earth Now, by the stout Schuylkill's beaver dam, if you dare to show your ugly, tory, cowboy, traitor heads in the streets of Philadelphia, after the Declaration is passed, I'll shoot you quicker than I would a squirrel. (*Raises his rifle*) Take your ugly face away from here, or I'll give you Bunker Hill! Go! (*Exit* 1 R. E.) Well, there goes a pretty pair of mongrel whelps. (*Crosses* R) Here comes some of the Congress men.

CONGRESSMEN *enter* 1. 1 E.   *Cross to door* F. *and go in.*

Crist. Buell, me darlint, whose these a coming here now, d'ye mind, up the street there ?

Buell. Them ? Sam Adams, the fire-brand, is one, and —yes, Tom Jefferson, George Reed, Dick Lee, Abe. Clark. Ed. Rutledge, and Ben Franklin. (*They enter in the above order, and go in door of* F) Hurray for the Continental Congress! hip! (*All cheer*) Grand things will be done to-day for the Colonies. (*To* CRIST) Did you see their eyes ? They're filled with a determined purpose.

Crist I did that, and be the powers of Saint Patrick I heard Tom Lynch, Jr., say there was fifty-six of them, and by me sowl I believe it will be the heaviest fifty-six that an Englishman ever attempted to lift. Whisht, boys, here comes more of them.

Buell. Stand back, there.   Make room to let them pass. (*As they enter*) That is Stephen Hopkins, the Quaker; there's William Hooper, John Penn, George Molton, John Adams, Richard Henry Lee, and Charles Carroll.

J ADAMS *enters door and returns to street.*

J. Adams. Come here, boy. (BOY *comes.*) You're a good Whig, ain't you ?

Boy. Yes, sir.   Father was at Bunker Hill.

J. Adams. Then I know you are the son of a patriot. You see that belfry ?   (BELLMAN *looks out.*)

Boy Yes, sir.

J. Adams. I want you to stand by that door, (*points off.*) and when the Declaration is signed we will tell you;

then you shout to the bellman to ring, and that will tell the people that the Declaration of Independence is pass d

Boy. I will, sir.

J. Adams. Remain firm at your post, for remember you are now a soldier of the revolution.

J. ADAMS *enters door and takes his seat in the hall.*

Buell Hurrah for the Continental Congress! Hip! hip! hip!
(*All cheer, then exit* R *and* L.)

SCENE II.—*Scene opens slowly. A low chord by or chestra—Yankee Doodle. Discovers interior of In dependence Hall* CONGRESSMEN *all seated* HANCOCK *just sitting down on right front. the Clerk's table on left raised platform, with desk for* HANCOCK. *On plet form sits* SAMUEL ADAMS, *in red suit On right sits* JEFFERSON. *in gent's suit of '76 A table below* HAN- COCK'S *desk with Declaration on it* HOPKINS *in Quak- er's garb stands up at rear of room with hat on. Over- head are two English flags crossed The whole form- ing a tableaux picture—Stewart's picture. Scene in Congress, July 4th,* 1776 *Tableaux for a few moments.*

Hancock. (*Strikes with the gavel*) Representatives wi'l come to order. Clerk, call the roll by States, and let one answer for their delegation.

Clerk. New Hampshire—Josiah Bartlett,William Whip- ple, Matthew Thornton.

Answered. Here.

Clerk. Massachosetts Bay — John Hancock, John Adams, Samuel Adams, Robert Treat Paine.

Ans. Here.

Clerk. Rhode Island—Eldridge Gerry, Stephen Hop- kins, William Ellery.

Ans. Here.

Clerk. Connecticut—Roger Sherman, Samuel Hunting- don, William Williams, Oliver Walcott.

Ans. Here.

Clerk. New York—Philip Livingston, Francis Lewis, William Floyd, Lewis Morris.

Ans. Here.

Clerk New Jersey—Richard Stockton, John Witherspoon, Francis Hopkinson, John Hart, Abraham Clark

Ans Here.

Clerk Pennsylvania—Robert Morris, Benjamin Rush, John Morton, Benjamin Franklin, George Clymer, James Smith, George Taylor, John Wilson, George Ross.

Ans. Here.

Clerk. Delaware—Cæsar Rodney, George Reed, Thomas McKean.

Ans. Here.

Clerk Maryland—Samuel Chase, Thomas Stone, William Paca, Charles Carroll

Ans. Here.

Clerk. Virginia—George Weyth, Richard Henry Lee, Thomas Jefferson, Benjamin Harrison, Thomas Nelson, Jr., Francis Lightfoot Lee, Carter Braxton.

Ans Here.

Clerk North Carolina—William Hooper, Joseph Hewes, John Penn.

Ans. Here.

Clerk. South Carolina—Edward Rutledge. Thomas Heywood, Jr., Thomas Lynch, Jr., Arthur Middleton.

Ans. Here.

Clerk. Georgia—Button Guinett, Lyman Hall, George Walton.

Ans Here.

Han. I now declare Congress in session; Clerk, read the minutes of yesterday's proceedings.

Clerk. State House, Philadelphia, Colony of Pennsylvania, North America, July 3d, 1776 Delegates met at 9 o'clock, A. M., Benjamin Harrison, of Virginia, in the chair. At roll call, fifty-six delegates answered. Robert R. Livingston, of New York, withdrew from the Convention. Minutes of July 2d read and approved. Congress opened again, in committee of the whole, to consider the Declaration under the following resolution, presented June 7th, by Richard Henry Lee: "Resolved, that these United Colonies are, and ought to be free and independent States, and all political connection between us and the States of Great Britain is and ought to be totally dis-

solved;" the same being seconded by John Adams-
Thomas Jefferson, John Adams, Benjamin Franklin and
Robert R Livingston were chosen a committee, to whom
was referred the whole subject; General Lee being omitted
from serving on the committee, at his own request. The
Declaration the committee presented was taken up *scria
tim*, and debated at length Among the many alterations
and erasures, the following was last ordered expunged:
"He, the King, determined to keep open a market, where
man should be bought and sold; He has prohibited his
negative for suppressing every legislative attempt to pro
hibit or restrain this execrable commerce; and that this
assembly of horrors might want no fact of distinguish d
die, he is now exciting those very people to rise in arms
amongst us, and to purchase that liberty of which *He* has
deprived them, by murdering the people upon whom he
also obtruded them; thus paying off forever, crimes com-
mitted against the liberties of one people, with crimes *He*
urges them to commit against the lives of another." At
the conclusion of which, Button Guinet, of Georgia, moved
to go into executive session, for the final adoption of the
Declaration. The House at half past four ordered an ad-
journment to July 4th, then to meet in regular session.

Han. (*Standing up*) Gentlemen—you have heard the
minutes of yesterday's Journal; any omissions or correc-
tions? (*pause*) If not, they will stand approved, as read.
(*Lets fall gavel*) So ordered. (*Sits down*)

Charles Carroll Mr. President—I now call for the
reading of that Declaration of Independence, as amended;
and sir, I would suggest as our worthy colleague, the
Hon. Benjamin Franklin, of Pennsylvania, was one of the
committee who drafted that instrument, he be requested
to read it.

Han. Will the gentleman of Pennsylvania be pleased
to comply with the request?

Benjamin Franklin. (*Steps to table below the President, takes up the document, and reads the* DECLARATION
OF INDEPENDENCE *Size of document must be quite large
written across the whole sheet and length of the paper,
with blank space below. During the reading of the Declaration, the* BELLMAN *shows considerable anxiety. The*

BELLMAN *looks anxiously below and around, after Declaration is read.*)

Bellman. (*To bell—shakes his head*) Old bell, it won't never be, that reading on your rim ain't for us. "Proclaim liberty throughout all the land, unto the inhabitants thereof?" No, it won't never be.

Richard Henry Lee. Mr. President.

Han Richard Henry Lee, of Virginia.

Lee. I now renew the motion made yesterday, on this floor, by the delegate from Georgia, that the Declaration just read be adopted.

J. Adams. I second that motion.

Han. (*Stands up*) It is moved by the delegate from Virginia, and seconded by the delegate from Massachusetts, that the Declaration just read be adopted; are you ready for the question? (*As* HOPKINS *speaks sits down*)

Stephen Hopkins Mr. President.

Han. Stephen Hopkins, of Rhode Island.

Hop. (*Spoken with deliberation.*) I trust our friends have well considered the importance of the step they are about to take; verily, we are friendless, and have no allies abroad to aid our cause; we may sink beneath the waves on which we are about to embark. This act will call down on us the vengeance of England's King. Would it not be better to defer the Declaration to some future period, for ye well know, in the beginning we aimed not to secure our Independence. Are there not yet hopes that the noble Chatham and Camden have prevailed upon the King and Parliament to extend us a more liberal policy? Ye should all solemnly reflect on the serious importance of this measure; but friends, if you do vote to adopt this Declaration of Independence, yea, verily, I will sink or swim with ye. My voice, my vote, is for this Declaration.

J. Adams. Mr. President.

Han. John Adams, of Massachusetts.

J. Adams. Sink or swim, live or die, survive or perish, I give my hand and heart to this vote. It is true, indeed, that in the beginning, we aimed not at Independence; but there is a divinity that shapes our ends. The injustice of England has driven us to arms; and, blinded to her own

interest, for our good she has obstinately persisted, until
independence is now within our grasp; we have but to
reach forth to it and it is ours   Why, then, should we
defer the Declaration?   Is any man so weak as now to
hope for a reconciliation with England, which shall leave
either safety to his own life or his own honor?   Are not
you, sir, who sit in that chair, is not he, our venerable
colleague near you, are you not both already the proscribed
and predestined objects of punishment and of vengeance?
Cut off from all hope of Royal clemency, what are you?
What can you be while the power of England remains,
but outlaws?   If we postpone Independence, do we mean
to carry on, or to give up the war?   I know we do not
mean to submit.   Do we mean to violate that most sol
emn contract ever entered into by men, that plighting before God, of our sacred honor to Washington, when put-
ting him forth to incur the dangers of war, as well as the political hazards of the times?   We promised to adhere to
him, in every extremity, with our fortunes and our lives.
I know there is not a man here who would not rather see
a general conflagration sweep over the land, or an earth-
quake sink it, than one jot or tittle of that plighted faith
fall to the ground.   For myself, having twelve months
ago, in this place, moved you that George Washington be
appointed Commander of the forces raised, or to be raised
for the defense of American liberty, "may my right hand
forget its cunning," "and my tongue cleave to the roof of
my mouth," if I waver or hesitate in the support I give
him.   The war, then, must go on; why put off longer the
Declaration of Independence?   That measure will strength-
en us; it will give us a character abroad, that cannot be
obtained while we acknowledge ourselves subjects in arms
against England's sovereign.   Nay, I maintain that Par
liament will sooner treat for peace with us, on the footing
of Independence, than consent, by repealing their acts,
to acknowledge that their whole conduct toward us has
been a course of injustice and oppression.   The former,
England would regard as the result of fortune; the latter,
she would regard as her own deep disgrace.   Our cause
will raise armies!   Our cause will create navies!   The
people, if we are true to them, will carry us, and will carry

themselves *gloriously* through this struggle. Sir, the Declaration will inspire the people with increased courage; instead of a long and bloody war, for restoration of privileges, for redress of grievances, for chartered immunities, held under a British King, set before them the glorious object of entire Independence, and it will breathe into them the breath of life. Read this Declaration at the head of the army; every sword will be drawn from its scabbard, and solemn vows uttered to maintain it, or to perish on the bed of honor. Publish it from the pulpit; religion will approve, and the love of religious liberty will cling around it, resolved to stand or fall with it. Send it to the public halls; proclaim it there; let them hear it who first heard the roar of the enemy's cannon; let them see it who saw their sons and their brothers fall on the field of Bunker Hill and in the streets of Lexington and Concord, and the very walls will cry out in its support. Sir, I know the uncertainty of human affairs, but I see clearly through this day's business. You and I, indeed, may not live to the time when this Declaration shall be made good; we may die Colonists, die slaves, die, it may be, ignominiously, and on the scaffold. Be it so, be it so; if it be the will of heaven that my country shall require the poor offering of my life, the victim shall be ready at the appointed hour of sacrifice, come when that hour may. But while I do live, let me have a country, or at least a hope of a country, and that a free country. But whatever is our fate, be assured this Declaration will stand; and it may cost blood but it will stand, and it will richly compensate for both. Through the thick gloom of the present, I see the brightness of the future, as the sun in heaven. We shall make this a glorious, an immortal day; when we are in our graves our children will celebrate it, with thanksgiving, with festivities, with bonfires and illuminations. On its annual return they will shed tears, copious, gushing tears, not of agony and distress, but of exultation, of gratitude and joy. Sir, before God, I believe the hour has come; my judgment approves this measure, and my whole heart is in it. All that I have I am now ready here to stake upon it; and I leave off as I began, that live or die, survive or perish, I am for the Declaration. It is my living sentiment, and by the blessing of God, it shall be my dying sentiment. *Independence now, and Inde pendence forever.*

Lee. Mr. President.

Han. Richard Henry Lee, of Virginia.

Lee. The time has certainly come, Mr. President, for the fated separation between the mother country and these Colonies. It is so decreed by the very nature of things. British injustice fills our hearts with indignation. Shall a foreign soil any longer regulate our domestic affairs ? Experience is the source of sage counsels, and Liberty is the mother of great men. Have you not seen the enemy driven from Lexington by a few armed men, and their experienced Generals defeated by a determined liberty-breathing patriots ? The very elements are in our favor. Then why do we longer delay—why still deliberate ? Let this most happy day give birth to the American Republic. Let her arise, not to devastate and conquer, but to re-establish the reign of peace and of the laws. The eyes of Europe are fixed upon us. She demands of us a living example of freedom, that may con ' trast, by the felicity of the citizens, with the ever increasing tyranny which desolates her polluted shores. She invites us to prepare ae asylum where the unhappy may find solace and the persecuted repose. She entreats us to cultivate a propitious soil, where that generous plant which first sprang up and grew in England, but is now withered by the poisonous blasts of tyranny, may revive and flourish, sheltering, under its salubrious and interminable shade, all the unfortunate of the human race. This is the end presaged by so many omens—by our first victories, by the present ardor and union, by the flight of Howe and the pestilence which broke out among Dunmore's people, by the very winds which baffled the eremy's fleets and transports, and that terrible tempest which engulfed seven hundred vessels on the coasts of Newfoundland. If we are not this day wanting in our duty to our country, the names of the American Legislators will be placed, by posterity, at the side of those of Theseus, of Lycurgus, of Romulus, of Nurna,, of the three Williams, of Nassau, and of all those whose memory has been and will be for-

ever dear to virtuons men and good citizens. Sirs, my
heart is set on the announcement of that Declaration to-
day.   The heart of every southern man true to the Colonies, and the whole interest of America, demands *that, as
a unit we live, as a unit we die?*   Dissolution from England *now!   A nation—one nation forever after*!

S. Adams. Mr President.

Han. Samuel Adams, of Massachusetts, sir-named the
Firebrand of the American Revolution.

S. Adams. Mr. President, such is the addenda, by the
people, to the gift of my father, and such, I hope, it will
descend to my children's children—"Samuel Adams, the
Firebrand of the American Revolution"—a title of nobility
I hope, that will be made patent by the announcement to-
day, that the Declaration of Independence has been unan
imously adopted.   My escutcheon shall grow the brighter
beneath the refulgent glow of a free people's happiness.
Our wrongs, my colleagues, you have heard.   How they
were thrust upon us we well know,   A partial account of
them is embraced in that Declaration.   How are they en-
dured ?   Groans and cries of misery come up in answer.
Now what sounds alarm your ears, and make your hearts
beat in hasty throbbings ?   The peal of musketry, the
boom of cannon, and the tramp of a foreign foe.   Above
all rise the cries of a people that *will* be free, *Liberty or
Death—Death or Liberty!*   Liberty from what ?   A tyranny of oppression the equal of which has not been since
Cæsar trod under foot our counterpart and prototypes,
the struggling Romans.   They had Rome and its forum—
we have the modern city of Philadelphia and the State
House of Pennsylvania.   The people whom we represent
are our spectators, and their plaudits will ring 'mid the
struggles of the battle-field.   The wreaths and bays will
come when peace and liberty sit at our people's firesides.
Sir, in this struggle I would turn incendiary.   Were there
a pyramid of thrones to confront me, and were the gran-
deur of their royalty and the powers of their scepters offered me, I would apply the sword of liberty as a torch
for their destruction, and watch to see the form of America arise frrom their ashes, around her the powerful trin-
ity of Liberty, Justice and Unity.   Clause after clause of

the original draft of that Declaration has been erased or
expunged, until the most simple statements of our wrongs
remain. The growing evil of the black man's slavery
(for all mankind loves freedom) we have consented to
omit, for the sake of unity, allowing the course of coming
event to work out the evil from among our children. Now
that the Declaration sets forth our simple wish of liberty
from a foreign thraldom, I feell that you will not fail to
strike, for the times demand it. Strike, for the people
expect it! Strike for *God and Liberty*.

   Thomas Jefferson Mr. President.

   Han. Thomas Jefferson, of Virginia

   Jefferson. Mr. President: Virginia urges on this De-
laration, her vote is for its adoption. Shall I repeat the
glaring injuries set forth in that Declaration, to induce
my brother colleagues to vote for its adoption? Do not
all the inhabitants, from the snow-clad hills of New York
to the burning plains of Georgia, cry out in agony for re-
lease from England's thraldom. Shall I recount the In-
dian astrocities inflicted upon our people? Those fiends
by whom the burning faggot was applied to pioneer's
homes while life yet lingered in their lacerated forms,
were led by British soldiery. Shall I turn to the mound
of Bunker Hill and bring the bleeding form of Warren,
with the long train of boys with the down of childhood
on their cheeks, and a mother's warm kiss on their fore-
desds; the sturdy form in the early glow of manhood,
who, but a few months since, sat at the home's fireside,
with children at his knee, to love and protect; the white-
haired ahd tottering form of eighty years, the father of
this line—shall I bring these forms, cold in death, from
the carnage of Bunker Hill, and pile them here in ghastly·
cords. and have them ask you to vote for this Declara-
tionb No! I feel I need not I see the cheeks of Northern men grow white, snd their bands clench with iron
energy. I see the warm blood flush on the glowing brow
and the fiery power of a slumbering volcano light up the
dark eye of Southern men, as if eager to start the labor-
ious work of building up this Temple of Liberty. It may
cost the blood that flows in our veins to cement the joints
of its workmanship. Let it cost. The Temple is worth

the sacrifice. A noble advocate for our cause has truly
said : "Three millions of people armed in the holy cause
of Liberty, in such a country as we possess, are invincible." Pass this Declaration, that the people may know
for what they shed their blood, and they will draw a giant's
power from the very soil on which they tread Is there
a heritage so great on earth as liberty ? Is there any
blessing so great as this, to bequeathe to our children ?
No! Sirs, there can be none. For ages to come, our de-
scendants will teach it to theirs, and the foundation stone
of this temple we lay to-day will grow to a massive pile,
and every crown that has tyranny for its scepter will grow
pale when the sun shines from the West, and casts its
shadow at their feet; it will face the East and West, the
North and South ; the verges of the Continent will alone
be its boundaries ; at its portals, standing guard, will be
our sons ; and their watchword will fill the heavens—*eternal vigilance is the price of liberty.*

Franklin. I call for the question !

Other Members. Question ! Question !

Han. The question is, upon the final adoption of the
Declaration of Independence. Mr. Clerk will call the
yeas and nays by States.

Clerk. New Hampshire.

Answers. Yea.

Clerk. Massachusetts.

Hancock Yea

Clerk. Rhode Island.

Hopkins. Yea, verily.

Clerk Connecticut.

Ans Yea.

Clerk. New York.

Ans Yea

Clerk. New Jersey.

Ans. Yea.

Clerk Pennsylvania.

Franklin. Yea.

Clerk. Delaware.

Ans. Yea.

Clerk. Maryland.

Ans. Yea.

Clerk. Virginia.
Ans. Yea.
Clerk North Carolina.
Ans. Yea.
Clerk. South Carolina.
Ans Yea.
Clerk Georgia.
Ans. Yea.
Clerk. Mr. President, the vote is unanimous.
Sam'l Adams (To Boy at window) It has passed.

Han I declare the vote unanimous, for the adoption of the Declaration of Independence Clerk, hand me the document. *(Signs it in a bold hand)* There! His Majesty, King George the Third, can read *that* without spectacles. Let him double his reward of a thousand pounds for my apprehension. I defy him!.

Voice. (Outside.) It has passed! Liberty! Freedom! Tyranny is dead!—Run hence, proclaim, cry it about the streets!

Boy. (Outside—shouts to BELLMAN*)* Ring! ring! ring!

BELLMAN *strikes bell six times as on shipboard: Bang! Bang!—Bang! Bang! Repeat People outside cheer. As the bell strikes, several Delegates come forward and sign.* STEPHEN HOPKINS *comes forward and signs*

John Adams Stephen Hopkins, you write with a trembling hand.

Hop. Ah! but John Bull will find I haven't got a trembling heart (ADAMS *signs.* JEFFERSON *signs.* CAR- ROLL *signs)*

Franklin Charles Carroll, you will escape, seeing there are so many of your name.

Carroll (Adds, "Of Carrollton.") Charles Carroll, of Carrollton If his majesty has any desire to find me, he can do so

Franklin. (Signs.) Now that we have signed this Dec- laration, we must all hang together, or—we will all hang separate.

(BELLMAN *strikes the bell two strokes three times. Con- gress sits in Tableau, as in the picture of signing the Declaration of Independence. The opening scene forms the same picture, only broken by the speakers. In Tab*

leau, BELLMAN *stands with hammer raised. People gath-*
er at each street with hats raised.)

Buell. (*Down on* L.) How many ages hence, shall this
lofty scene be recounted over, in States unborn and ac-
cents yet unknown?

Otis (*R.*) So long as sun will shine, so long shall this
knot (*Pointing to Signers*) be called "The men that gave
their country liberty."

(*The two English flags at end of hall part, showing
Goddess of Liberty. Red or blue fire. Music, "Hail
Columbia." Slow curtain.*

ACT III.

SCENE 1.—*Winter quarters at Valley Forge.* 5 *G.*
Log Hut, R. between 4 and 5. *Door on side, Stack of
Arms in front. and L. of door. Camp Fire in front of
Stack Sentinel pacing beat across stage. Drummer in
front of hut beating "Sick Call."* CRIST *comes out of
hut wrapped in old blanket. Stage dark.*

Crist. Turn out! Turn out! and pay your morning
visit to the doctor. This is a devil of a cold morning to
be turning the poor, starved creatures out. They have
narry a whole shoe, nor hat, nor coat, nor shirt in the
whole company. Some of the poor creatures will have
to lay in their straw until their hunkeys return from the
hospital, so they can get the lind of a pair of pants. Turn
out, and get your quinine!—if the Doctor has any.

(*Enter* DOCTOR LINCOLN, *L., with medicine chest and
camp stool, takes a seat near fire. Sentinel salutes.*)

Doc. Good morning, Sergeant.

Crist. (*Aside*) The new Doctor, knows my name.

Doc I will spare your poor men the trouble to go to
the hospital this cold morning, half clad as they are.

Crist. Indeed, Doctor, you are doing the sinsible thing.
The poor creatures would be all morning getting the loan
of clothes from one another to visit ye.

Doc Are they as destitute of clothing as all that Sargeant?

Crist. Faith, they are; wait till you see them.   Come, turn out, boys! the Doctor brought the hospital right foreinst your doors.   Answer to your names, and come out as I call them off the sick list.   *(Culls from book)* "Patrick Kelly."

(Voice within) "Here."

Crist. That poor creature hasn't been able to do duty for a month for want of shoes.

(Enter soldier, poorly clad and barefooted, goes to Doctor who prescribes.)

Crist. (Calls) "Jacob Krout."

(Voice Within.) Say, Sargeant. I don't got some pants ɔ come by the Doctor, yoost now.

Crist. Well, why the divil don't ye borrow a pair from the other Dutchman, as usual?

Doc. (To soldier.) I'll excuse you from duty until you get some shoes. *(Exit soldier.)*

                    Enter Krout.

Well, my man, what's the matter with you?

Krout. What's ter matter mit me?   Dat's told putty quick; I feel me so hungry dat I go *kap put* putty soon —odder I freeze me to dead.   It makes me nodings out ob one or the onder one come furst, odder both come furst, I don't care putty much.   I can stand one yoost so gute as the ander one, and a tam site better too, dats wats ter matter mit me.   I feel me mad mit der Congress.

Doc. If that is all, my dear fellow, I'll excuse you from duty until you get food and clothes, which are expected daily.

Krout. I don't got some duty to do—I was a Lieutenant.   *(Re enters hut.)*

Crist. (Calls.) "Jeffrey Sparks."

Voice within. Sergeant, he's too weak to leave his bunk.

Crist. (Calls) "Thomas Henderson."

Voice within Sargeant, he's stiff and cold these two hours.

Crist. Doctor, your prescription will do him no good. I feared all along he wouldn't see the outside of Valley Forge again.   Peace be to his soul! *(Calls.)* "Patrick

Devine, Hans Sneider, Julius Cæsar Smith, Billy Patter-
son, Alexander Hannibal"—Doctor, they are all book d
for the other hospital; they'll follow in the wake of poor
Thomas Henderson. Doctor, we have a patient that you
must see, whether or no. He's cooking for the boys,
when he can get anything to cook, and, of course, as soon
as we draw rations the cook must be in good trim for
business. Boys, a couple of yees lead out our colored
friend, Sampson Foster, till the Doctor makes a post mor-
tem examination of his black carcass. (KROUT *and a soldier lead out* SAMPSON, *who looks very weak. Doctor
gives him stool.*)

Doc. Sampson, (*feeling of pulse,*) you are too poorly
to remain in your quarters; you must be removed to the
hospital.

Krout. Yaw, dat is what I tole him.

Samp. I isn't gwine to the hospital, dat's sure death.
If I must die, let me lay down here, mid my feet to the
fire, and I is satisfied.

Crist. We'll not allow you to do that again, Sampson.
The last time you laid wid your feet ferninst the fire you
burnt the soles off of the only decint pair of shoes in Valley Forge, that you had the lind of. Would you now
burn the soles of your big fate, too?

Samp. I declare to goodness, Massa Crist, I can't stand
it much longer. I believe I is gwine to meet the good
Lord pretty soon, fire or no fire at my feet.

Krout. (*Holding* SAMP. *up.*) Was ish dat? You was
to go by the Lord, and mit your feets down by the fire?
(*Meditating*) Oh, now I see what you mean. When you
was going down, (*Pointing down,*) and your feet come
by das fire, you right away quick jumps up to the Lord,
(*Pointing up.*) I guess I dry me dat too when my time
was come

Doctor. (*To* CRIST) I don't think he will stand it much
longer—See, he is getting weaker—I am afraid he is past
my help.

Crist We'll see if he has made his peace with his good
Lord—maybe he has a dying request to make. Say,
Sampsom, my good lad, can we do anything for ye—what
is your last request on this earth?

Sampson. (*Pause.*) Oh, Massa Christ, give me a chaw tobaccer.

Crist. Well, did you ever hear the like of that? Could the heathen go to meet his God with a chew tobacco in his mouth—he'd better be asking for a Priest.

Doc. Remove him, men! and give him an easy bed. (SAMPSON *carried off.*)

Crist. Yes, remove him—(*Aside*) It will bother their brains to get a soft bed in this camp. The soft side of the hard frozen ground, wid a bit of straw, but nary a blanket—O, we have another patient, Doctor,—our Captain, Seth Peabody. The poor fellow has been sick these two months, he's scarcely able to walk, (*Looking to L.*) but I see he is out this morning, and coming this way.

Doc. Captain Seth Peabody! Why, I knew him in Boston.

Crist. Did you, and are yees from Boston? Faith, I thought I knew you—How do you do, Doctor Lincoln! Boston is the first place I landed at in America. We are all Boston boys, here. (*Shaking hands.*)

Enter SETH, L. 2 E.

Doc. Captain Peabody, I am glad to see you, but sorry to see you looking so miserable.

Seth. Doctor, I am glad to see you. How were all the folks down in Boston when you left? We are all kinder miserable here, and if I had my health I'd walk right through that Continental Congress, and wake 'em up, unless they furnish us more clothes, and provisions, and money, and everything else we need to keep the poor soldiers alive. Why, they are dying off here like sheep with the hoof-rot. I was boiling over with patriotism, and all that sort of thing, about the time of the Lexington and Bunker Hill fights. The fight is clear out of me now; I am done fighting for glory—I want something to exercise my jaws on.

Crist. Yes, Captain, we all want something. If we were only back in Boston now what a time we would have eating baked beans and pork and Boston brown-bread, wid a good pot of ginger beer, or something a little stronger, to wash it down wid.

Doc. Gentlemen, your wants in that respect will be

soon supplied. General Washington is doing his utmost to hurry supplies to the army, but that Congress that is always doing something in the wrong time, has relieved Colonel Trumbull from the head of the Quartermaster and Commissary Department, and thereby deranged the whole system of procuring supplies, and the few supplies on hand can not be forwarded on account of the bad condition of the road.

Seth. If it wasn't for our great General, we'd be marching to Congress and deranging their whole system for 'em, bad roads wouldn't stop us.

Crist. Faith, they would not. Bad 'cess to 'em. (*Doctor prescribes for* SETH *and* SETH *retires.*)

Doc Sergeant, you say you are all Boston boys here. Well, if so, you can probably inform me where I can find one Buell Pomeroy?

Crist. Buell, is it; faith, I can.

Doc. I have a valuable letter for him from Miss Rose.

Crist You have a letter for him, from Rose Creighton —sure, that's just whats ailing him all along. He is the chap that went for the soldiers in Boston, at the massacre where Miss Rose's little brother Willie was killed in cold blood, by them blood-thirsty devils. That British officer, Captain Preston, stands in bad boots, if Buell ever meets him, for he swore to kill him *wherever* he met him. Buell took the little boy's body home to Rose and her sister Kate, and he saw them taking on so bad, so he came back to the boys—who were wid him in the row—got down on his knees, and such another oath you never heard a mortal man make. Ever since then I never valued that Captain's skin worth a sixpence.

Doc. I have learned that the Misses Creighton are much obliged to him for a great deed of kindness, consequently are much interested in his welfare. Where is he; can you send for him here, Sergeant?

Crist. That I kin, Doctor. (*Goes to Hut.*) Corporal Dunningan, go down to Colonel Frazier's quarters, and tell Major Buell Pomeroy that the new Doctor from Boston sinds his compliments, and wants to see him here immediately, if not sooner. (*Returning to the Doctor.*) You see, Doctor, Buell has been promoted to Major by

General Washington, and he has as fine a set of scouts under his command as ever straddled horses. They ca' them the "Riders of the Santee." The Scouts they always turn up at the right time, wherever they are wanted. B t here comes the gentleman himself He is a little under the weather, like the rest of us, but that letter from M'ss Rose will cure him.

Ente, BUELL L.. 2 E.

Doctor Lincoln, Major Buell Pomeroy—Major Pomeroy, Doctor Lincoln. (*They shake hands.*) (*Aside*) O' . I'll get used to American manners soon.

Buell. I am happy to meet you, Doctor; I learn you are just from Boston.

Doc Yes, Major, I am just from Boston, and I have been entrusted with this letter (*presenting it*) by Miss Rose Creighton, and I feel sure its perusal by you w'' drive away the gloomy thoughts and surroundings, and for the time forget you are in Valley Forge

Buell. A thousand thanks to you, Doctor. Pray excuse me. (*Retires up—Reads.*)

Crist. Doctor.

Doc. Well, Sergeant?

Crist. I don't feel very well myself this morning. (*Playing off sick.*) What have you in the black bottle there?

Doc. In this bottle? (*Holding it up.*) This is only used in extreme cases (*Smiling*)

Crist. I think this is an extreme case then. I feel o sick. I'm on the top of the sick list, too.

Doc. You may take a little of it, then, if you are so sick (*Giving bottle.*)

Crist. God bless you, sir. (*Takes a long pull*)

Doc. Sergeant! Sergeant, (*taking bottle from him,*) that will do.

Crist. Yes, Doctor, but I feel so bad. Another swig of it will cure me.

Doc. Touch it lightly, Sergeant. (*Giving bottle*)

Brist. Thank you, Doctor, I feel better now. But Doctor, you don't look altogether well this morning; you look pale; hadn't you better take a bit of the creature, too?

Doc. Oh, no, thank you, Sergeant, I think not.

Crist. Oh, well, of course you know best—you are the Doctor. (*Wiping his mouth.*)

BUELL *comes down ; Two soldiers come out of Hut and shake a blanket;* KROUT *comes out, shakes his tattered and torn piece of a blanket very gently, and then looks at it, making some remark ; the first two go in and another soldier comes out, with an armfull of straw ; he shakes it up, and then goes in ;* KROUT *follows.*

Doc Cheering news, I presume, Major ?

Buell Yes, Doctor, the mail is the soldiers only friend in these blustering times of war.

Doc. Especially when the mail is from a dear female. (*Watching* BUELL *closely*)

Buell. Yes, I see by this note that the carrier can truly read ; how I welcome such tidings. I can speak freely to you now ; and first, allow me to congratulate you for being the accepted suitor of Miss Kate Creighton, a most estimable lady.

Doc I can return the compliment, and I pray you, Major, accept my congratulations for being the accepted suitor of her sister, Miss Rose Creighton, who is worthy of your generous love. (*Distant shouts heard*—DOCTOR *and* BUELL *listen.*)

Crist. (*Aside.*) I suppose they will be brothers in-law, soon—husbands to a fine pair of girls at that. That makes me think. (*Scratching his head*) When will I ever see my sweet Kathleen ? (*Distant shouts heard*)

Doc. (*Looking off L.*) What means this shouting ?

Buell. I think Washington is walking through the camp, encouraging the soldiers. Their love for him is preventing mutiny and wholesale desertion from this pen of death. (*Shouts come closer*—"*All soldiers turn out of quarters*")

Enter WASHINGTON *from L. 2 E., dressed in large cloak—Snowing.*

Omnes. Huzza ! Long live Washington !

Wash. Cheer up, brave men, I am aware of your suffering condition ; clothing and provisions will soon be in camp. Be calm and obedient to your officers, insubordination will result only in evil—think of the cause you are engaged in.

Soldier. General, we know our conduct has been mutinous, but our condition justified it. We are actually starving, and relief must be had. We were going to march out in an orderly manner into the country, seize provisions wherever they could be found, giving in return certificates as to the amount and value of articles taken, and then return to camp, and to our duty.

Wash. It grieves me to the heart to see you thus, but I am straining every nerve to obtain relief.

Soldier. General, we know you are our friend. Congress is to blame for our condition; we are starving her and shall soon be of no service to you or our country. We love you and the cause in which we are embarked. We will stand by you at all hazards, and defend with our last drop of blood our common country, but food we must and will have. (*Going down R*)

Wash. (*Much moved*) My faithful soldiers, I admire the manly grounds you take in defense of your conduct. I have long admired your patience, resignation and devotion to your country under these most trying circumstances, and if the provisions do not arrive by a certain time I will place myself at your head, and march into the country, until they are found.

Omnes. Long live George Washington!

Soldier. God bless you, General!

Wash. I have issued a proclamation, in which I have ordered all farmers within seventy miles of Valley Forge to thresh out half of their grain by the first of February, and the other half by the first of March, under penalty of having the whole seized as straw

Sold. These Tory farmers are worse than our enemy.

Wash. My gallant men, I have good tidings for you— our cause looks brighter. General Gates and his brave army in the North succeeded in hemming in the enemy's entire army under Lieut. Gen Burgoyne, and compelled it to surrender on very favorable terms.

Omnes. Hurrah! hurrah! (*Shouting—Guns*)

Wash. The overthrow of Burgoyne will fix the wavering attitude of France, and a treaty of defensive alliance, as well as of amity and commerce in all probability can now be arranged without a doubt.

Omnes. Long live the King of France! Long live La Fayette! (*Loud shouting.*)

Wash. An alliance with France, one of the strongest powers on the globe, will assure the success of the American arms.

Omnes. "The American States," and "Long live Washington."

SCENE 11—*Landscape*, 2 *G*, *Enter* GENERALS CONWAY' GREENE *and* COLONEL FRAZER, *R*

Greene. Well, gentlemen, we seem to have reached pretty near the crisis at last.

Conway. Yes, thanks to the Fabian policy of our illustrious General.

Greene. Conway, desist! for shame! Will you never have philosophy enough to conceal your envy?

Con. Envy!

Greene Yes, envy! We are all aware of the machina tions of yourself, Gates and Lee aided by your adherents in Congress; and for what? because you were disappointed in your ambition to become Chief!

Con. Such language to me! General Greene?

Greene. Aye, to you! and I tell you, to your teeth, the hero whom you secretly plot against, you would no more dare to bandy words with openly, than you would to snatch the cubs from a hungry lioness! Thank heaven on your knees for his magnanimous heart, which is so full of overflowing with anxiety for his country's redemption, he has no room to house a single thought upon such malignant, secret schemers!

Con. You wrong me, Greene, I yield to no man in my loyalty to my country, and to him that it has chosen to be its chief.

Greene. Ah! There's where the shoe pinches. Let your loyalty be shown in deeds as well as words. Remember the strait we are now in, our force reduced by many thousands, with a vast army, heaven knows how near to us at this moment. What would be the result should it arrive unexpectedly?

Con. A short one—utter annihilation !

Greene. Not so Conway. Be our position never so desperate, I have abundant faith in his resources, whose profound sagacity, unwearied zeal and wondrous general-ship indicate that he is even by the hand of Providence marked out to be the saviour of his country !

(Col. Frazier *looking off, L*)

Fraz. Yonder is our illustrious General in a secluded spot down on his knees—a duty we are want to perform. See, he lifts his eyes toward heaven and begins to pray. Listen ! (*All look off L*)

Washington (*without, praying in a loud voice*) Oh, Father ! Let the humblest of thy servants beseech Thee that war may pass from this land ! In the battle, in tri umphs and in defeat, I have called upon Thee, and heard Thine answer in the death cry and the battle shout ! I beseech Thee to crown the efforts of our weak but noble army with success in battling for our righteous. Grant that the malcontents in the halls of our Continental Con- gress and those in the ranks of our army (*Conway much moved*) be reconciled to their duty and by their united efforts deliver our country from the hands of our foreign foe.

Greene. He bows his head in silent prayer; (*pause*) no, he rises and comes this way.

Enter Washington, *L with papers.*

All. The General ! (*Saluting*)

Wash. Gentlemen, I cannot conceal from you, for it is self-evident, that we are in imminent peril. Our small, but brave and noble army, broken down by privations, has almost arrived at the limit of endurance, and at this moment with its energies paralized, and hope almost quenched, the enemy with fiendish ingenuity, has caused this proclamation, offering pardon and protection to all who may lay down their arms, to be scattered through our ranks ; and with profound grief I am compelled to say that there are not wanting those, even in our very coun- cils, who do not disfavor this unmanly and infamous al- ternative ! (*Tears paper*) If there be one amongst us, who even in thought, subscribed to this unworthy offer, let him at once depart, and carry with him the mark of Cain upon his forehead, and be forever pointed at as the traitorous slaver of his country's liberty.

Con. I'll answer with my life, there is no such man amongst us.

Wash. I'm glad to hear *you* say so General Conway, and in thus offering, in all sincerity, my hand to a brave, honorable soldier, forget forever the slanderous whispers which have reached my ears. I cannot err in supposing that a sense of justice will banish from *his* heart, also, the degrading doubts, and evil thoughts, engendered there by others, whose poor malignity and selfish aim must, in the end recoil upon themselves, for, while I am actuated by no hope beyond the weal of our beloved land. I wear an armor so invincible, the petty shafts of malice fall upon it harmless as the summer's rain.

Con. Sir, you have both shamed and conquered me. I do confess that I have listened, but too greedily, to accusations levelled at your fair fame. I cast them from me now, utterly and forever. To doubt the sacredness of your mission, would be to doubt heaven itself! Henceforward both with heart and hand, in word and act, I am entirely yours. Pardon but the past and as I live, the future shall atone.

Wash. Enough, my friend, all is forgotten but our duty to our country. Has any one ascertained the movements of the enemy?

Greene. Not with certainty. The common report is that they are evacuating Philadelphia and mean to give up battle; but the intermediate country is so disaffected to our cause, we cannot rely upon our information.

Wash. I have not received any information of their plans, but I have been reliably informed that a number of Tory spies have been for weeks within our lines, watching the effect of General Lord Howe's Proclamation, taking beside, very careful observations of our ill-provided army. The execution of a spy would have a wholesome effect.

Fraz. General, there may be some truth then of the enemy's intention to draw us out into battle. They may know of our defenceless position and advance their army, and—

Wash. Even then I would not despair. My neck does'nt

feel as if it was made for a halter. No, gentlemen. if the God of battles in the wisdom of his Providence, should avert his aid from the cause of humanity, we will make our last stand here—this shall be our Thermopylæ of Freedom, when its Spartan defenders will achieve immortality even through the medium of defeat and death! (*Gun eeard outside   Alarm Drum*) What means this tumult in the camp? I hope it is not a surprise. (*Loud laughter outside*) The surprise does not seem to be a harmful one. Now, Orderly!

Enter, ORDERLY. *L.*

Orderly. A prisoner, General.

Wash. By whom captured?

Orderly. I do not know, sir, Captain Seth Peabody has him in charge.

Enter, SETH, *L with* CURRY, *guarded by sentinel.*

Wash. What means this tumult in camp?

Seth I beg a million pardons for the boys, kase they all feel sorter good, General, to see this fellow catched, and they persuaded me to bring the chap afore you. You may want to know something about him.

Wash. Who is he, and what has he been doing?

Seth. My Sergeant says he is a Spy.

Curry. General, I deny the charge.   I am a resident of Philadelphia.

Wash. That would not prevent you from being a spy upon the Americans.(*To* SETH) Was he caught within our ''nes?

Seth. Major Buell's scouts caught him prowling about our lines.   They arrested and searched him, and found these papers on his person.(*giving papers*) They brought him into camp and said my sergeant can cook his goose for him (CURRY *very uneasy*) andhurried off again to join 'he Major.   Here comes the Sergeant.

Enter CRIST, *R*

Wash. Sergeant, what do you know about this man?

Crist. Please your honor, Gineral, 'tis I that knows Mr. Jeems Curry.   He is a bad egg. He's a dirty, skeaming ould villain.   The devil and him only knows what he's been up to these last ten years.   He is the very chap that was contriviving to kidnop the Adamses and Hancock up at Boston a few years ago. Faith, he followed them down to Philadelphia. Major Buell and myself were sint there wid papers for the Congress, and the very day the Declaration was passed, my laddy-buck was on the streets, saying he was a free-born English subject, and all that sort of blarney, and that he'd like to see the Continental Congress, General Washington, and all the rest of us hung.

Wash. (*Perusing Papers*) These papers found on your person are sufficient evidence of your being a spy. (*Observing him*) Yes, I also recognize in your countenance that villainous guide, who was to take General Braddock to Fort Du Quesne, but led us into an ambush. Captain, place him under a strong guard.

(*Exeunt* SETH, SENTINEL and CURRY *L*)

Crist. You'll die with your brogans on you. (*Follows off.*)

Wash Gentlemen these papers are very important to us. The delay of an hour would be fatal to our existence. The enemy has planned an attack, and Major Buell informs me that he can frustrate it; but, we must guard against a surprise. I will therefore, summon a council of war, and determine on a movement of the army. *You* Colonel, must also be present.

Fraz. Your Excellency, I'm not much of a hand at planning. I like to have my work laid out for me. When I know I have *so* much fighting to do 'and *so* many minutes to do it in, I can go right about it. You just plan an attack on Tartarus, and I'll undertake to storm the gates.

Greene. But, Colonel, the General desires your presence.

Wash. I must have your opinion, Colonel. Too much responsibility rests upon us, to justify a superficial consideration of our course of action. (*Exeunt L*)

QUICK CHANGE.

SCENE III—*5th G. Battle Ground of Monmouth; Discharge of musketry is kept up behind wings;* CONTINENTALS *retreating in confusion across stage from L to R ;* COL FRAZIER *endeavoring to stay the retrea'*
Enter WASHINGTON *from R.*

Wash. (In a rage) Hold! men! for shame! Are you the men I am to defend America with? Colonel, what means this conduct?

Fraz. Sir, General Lee is in full flight and disorderly retreat.

Wash. Full flight, from what?

Fraz. Fleeing from a mere shadow.

Enter more CONTINENTALS *from L , reloading, among them a wounded standard bearer.* WASHINGTON *takes his colors.*

Wash. Rally around me, this day will yet be ours! (CONTINENTALS *appe ir at R wing under* SETH) (*To* FRAZIER) Colonel, I depend on your men to check this : treat. (*Cheers*) Now, soldiers, this important hour may decide our country's fate; may the guiding star of American liberty this day lead us to another victory. Think of your homes, your mothers, wives and children! I" you do not follow, here shall I find my grave, for not one inch will I retreat.

Omnes On! on! Long live Washington!

Enter eight BRITISH SOLDIERS. *L . commanded by* PRESTON. *Both Armies keep up a orisk fire Music.*

A Voice from Continental Side. Reinforcements are coming!

Another Voice. Hurrah for Major Buell and the Riders of the Santee! (*Bugle sounds a charge; loud shouting.*)

Wash Forward! guide centre, charge!

(CONTINENTALS *move forward to L , led by* WASHINGTON *At same time enter* BUELL *from R 1 E with 5 Ride. who file across stage, backs to audience, and fire* BUELL *and* PRESTON *behold each other and they run and cross swords.* CONTINENTALS *drive* BRITISH *off L. and the Riders make a "right wheel" and follow.* BUELL *and* PRESTON *spring apart and take distance*)

Prest. (*Aside*) I feel my hour has come; I would sooner have met the devil himself than him

Buell Preston, I'll now fulfill the oath I made over the bodies of my countrymen, whom you massacred in cold blood at Boston, and avenge their deaths, or die in the attempt.

Prest. Sir, and I have longed to meet you; now make your vaun.ings true.

Buell. With all my heart; your life or mine. Come!

(*They advance and fight. Music.* PRESTON *wounds* BU-ELL, *and* BUELL *kills* PRESTON *During the combat en-ter* SETH, CRIST, KROUT, *and* SAMPSON ; *when* PRESTON *falls they shout, and*

C.. nes The day is ours.

> PICTURE.   RED FIRE.

SAMPSON.   KROUT.   CRIST.   SETH.
> BUELL.
> PRESTON.

QUICK DROP AND RISES ON TABLEAU—"SURRENDER OF HESSIANS TO WASHINGTON."
> CURTAIN.

ACT IV.

SCENE I—*Parlor, 4, G , Door in C.; Dressing stand and settees on R. and L ; Upholstered chairs to suit; Marble-top centre table; Basket of cut flowers.* ROSE *discovered on R. and* KATE *on L. of table, making wreathes and bouquets. C. D. open, and backed by landscape; carpet on stage.*

Kate. Sister Rose, why do you look so sad? Surely to-day above all others since the Declaration of Peace, you should feel as gay and happy as our returning heroes feel, who are to be welcomed to our city and crowned with wreathes and flowers on their homeward journey.

Rose Dear Kate, I know our heroes will feel gay and happy to day as they march through under the Triumphal Arch, their path strewn with flowers, and with the thought of being met on the other side of it by loving wives, and sisters, and kindred dear. How gladly would we welcome and enfold our arms around a kindred, but God in His wisdom has bereft us of all blood relations. To think that our dear soldiers, who have for years battled for Liberty and our Homes will this day have a Gala-Day, cheers me; but, remember, dear sister, to day is also the anniversary of brother Willie's death.

Kate. I know it, [*pause*] but I did not wish to speak of it. We will ever rememder the woful day; his bleeding form was laid at our feet on that memorable morn in Boston. But as he is past all worldly care, and gone to meet our father and mother in Heaven, I have long since yielded due submission to our Creator, and you should. too

Rose. I have. Still we are left alone in this world, no brother nor sister, and I sometimes think we are entirely friendless and forsaken.

Kate. Come, cheer up, Rose; we are not entirely friendless: remember, I am soon to have a brother, and one doubly dear to you and me since he is the avenger of Willie's death,—and besides, he will some day make you happy. There, you are looking sad again!

Rose. Yes, and I feel sad for him. Remember, by avenging the death of our brother—through no other motive but to see justice meeted out to the perpetrator of the horrid deed—our noble friend Buell Pomeroy came near losing his own life when he met that villain Capt, Preston face to face at the battle of Monmouth, and while in deadly combat with him was dangerously wounded.

Kate. Don't borrow more trouble; the Major has fully recovered from his wounds through your kind nursing while on furlough. I am waiting patiently to see the day when he will be your—that is, my brother-in law. Recollect, with the declaration of peace dates your unconditional surrender to him as a prisoner, to be led to Hymen's Altar.

Rose. Let us change the subject for the present, or I

may retort with the same weapons upon some one who is running a narrow escape from being captured in the same way Don't you think we have bouquets enough—all we can carry?

Kate. Perhaps we have. Dear me; I would wish we could present each color-bearer in the line with a wreath, and every soldier with a bouquet. [*Holding up a bouquet*] Isn't that a pretty one? I'll reserve this for the Boston Boy I see passing by in the ranks. (*Bell rings.*) There goes the bell,—why, how forgetful we are,—'tis already ten o'clock; the hour Major Pomeroy was to call to accompany us down street to witness the Grand Entre of the troops into the city.—I'll go to the door. (*Exits C. D*)

Rose. (*Going to glass, arranging toilet and goes to window*) The Major is punctual, and with him comes Dr. Lincoln. That accounts for Kate's cheerfulness this morning. (*Goes to C. D.*)

(*Enter* BUELL *C. D. from L. followed by* KATE *escoring* DOCTOR LINCOLN.

Rose. I am so delighted to see you, Major. (*Taking him by the hand*) Good morning, Doctor. (*Courtesies.*)

Doctor Good morning, Miss Creighton.

Rose This is a lovely May morning for the army to march through our city, is it not? The rain early this morning layed the dust nicely, and, besides, it kept the flowers on the Grand Arch, and those decorating the houses along the line of march, more fresh.

Buell. This is really a beautiful morning,—the air is cool and scented with the rich perfume of the flowers so liberally strewn on the streets. A soldiers' march is seldom bedded with flowers, and lined with glad and smiling faces as their march this morning will be.

Kate. (*Coming down to table.*) We were so busily engaged making these wreaths and bouquets (*all come down to table*) to present to the soldiers, and talking of one thing and another, (*Rose, uneasy.*) that Rose was almost forgetting your your promised call. Doctor, of course you will do us the honor to accompany the Major and us to see the grand entree of General Washington and the Army?

Doc. Certainly. Nothing will afford me more pleasure. Miss Creighton. I am at your services.

Rose. (*Pinning a nosegay on* BUELL's *coat.*) Major, what hour does the march begin ?

Buell. For eleven o'clock, it is ordered. 'Tis near that now.

Kate. (*Pinning a nosegay on the* DOCTOR) There, Doctor, let it not be said that we show any partiality in *this* house.

Doc. No fear of that, Miss Creighton. Your frankness bespeaks the two generous nature of its occupants.

Kate. No flattery, Doctor.

Doc. Where there's truth, there's no flattery.

Kate. Indeed !.

Rose. Don't shower too many compliments on each other over them.

Kate. Oh, we are not indulging in any, never fear.

Buell. Ha, ha, Kate, you may as well, 'twould he pardonable in your case. You forget that we may possibly be in the secret of the pledged *to-be* relationship of the parties in that side tete a-tete.

Kate. No more of that, Major,—let's change the subject.

Rose. Ah, ha ! my girl, I see you do not like to be paid in your own coin.

Doc. How do you account for that, Miss Rose ?

Rose. Well,—I'll spare her this time

Kate. Oh, you may speak out; it is not me you will spare, 'tis yourself I've not surrendered yet. (*All laugh at* ROSE *but* DOCTOR.)

Doc. (*Aside*) I'll not give up the seige.

Buell. Ladies, we must he moving, 'tis drawing near the hour. Doctor, let us help pack the bouquets in the basket. (KATE *helps.*)

Rose. Yes, do, gentlemen. Kate, hurry and put on your hat. Never mind looking for that particular bouquet for the Boston Boys,—we will find it.

(ROSE *and* KATE *go to settees and get hats. Band at back of stage playing a martial air, as if at a distance*)

Kate. Hark ! the troops are on the march.

Doc Oh, we will be in time to see the head of the col-
umn pass.

(*Takes basket. Exit C. D.*)

CHANGE.

SCENE II.—*Street* 1 *G. Enter* SETH *L in Captain's full
uniform;* KROUT *in a Lieutenant's;* SAMPSON *in an officers old uniform, and* CRIST *in a Sergeant's uniform.*

Crist. Hould on, ye black divil! Would yer plaze take
yer position iu the rear of me? (*Throws him to back of
him*) Faith, the people would think ye out-ranked me
case ye have an officers old uniform on ye. Mind ye, I
am a full-blown Sergeant, with a certificate of disability
in my pocket, but divil a one have you, I know.

(SETH *assumes a dignified attitude*)

Samp. Who's you jerking around? Isn't we all discharged on leave of absence for a couple of hours? What
did General Washington tell us de oder day? Didn't he
tell you all to treat us soldiers brodderly?

Krout. Sashant, Sashant! I put you on a rest, look
oud! De peoples dink we was all loafers fighting on de
shtreet.

Seth. That unmannerly conduct reflects consarned little
credit on your Capting, and right square in the presence of
him, too. Didn't I larn you better nor that in the last
seven years of soljering?

Crist. Of course ye did, Captain, and the beast should
have more dacency. Sure, we all wants to take a peace-
able walk through the city before we leave for Boston.
Do ye's mind the pretty flowers Miss Rose flung at me
when we came marching in the city this morning?

Krout. Yaw, yaw, dat was pretty nice, just so nice like
mine, von the same ladies—

Samp You see, we is all Boston Boys, and Massa
Buell and the Doctor knowed us, and dat's the case we
all is so kivered up with garlands.

Seth You're righ there, them gals were just looking
for us too. I promised the Major we would all call and
pay our respects to to him before we cleared out for

hum. Well, boys, what did you think of the turn out of York State ladies anybow? Wasn't there some busters out, this morning?

Krout. Chiminy-krout! dat was so, Captain,—some pretty nice gals was by der shtreet, mit nice, ret cheeks just like he got 'em in Germany.

Sump. Did yer,—did yer see dat nice yeller gal down on the corner selling ice cream? She thought I was an ossifer, and took my hands, and said, "How-de" to me, and treated me to a mess of dat cream. Golly, wasn't it nice?

Crist. Pwhat de divil do we know about it? Sure, we had none. But lads, did ye's see me leave the ranks after we passed through the big bow—that arch—where all the young ladies and little girls stood, dressed in white?

Seth. Sergeant, did you leave the ranks without my permission? I'll have you court-marshaled for desertion?

Crist. Och, Captain, sure I had the ould pass, the French one,—but hould on, don't bother me again till I tell the story. Well, in the crowd, I thought I saw one of the gurls from the "Ould Sod" I knew; and, sure enough, it was. She axed me down to her ould mother's place, and I went, of course, and as I went in the door I saw a little pine bar forninst me, and a sign overhead wid "No Trust" on it. The girl tould her ould mother I was an Irish lad after her own heart, (*Aside*—"*that's a lie.*") and that I should have a drop of the best stuff in the shanty. (*Aside —that's another.*) I got it; and wid my blessings on their heads, I left them, and I stepped back into the ranks.

Krout. Well, das was all ride, Captain, dat was desertion back again by der company.

Seth. Well, boys, what are you going to do when you all get discharged? Plague-on me, I can't tell what will become of us, if Congress don't do something for us. The pension won't be much, and if it would, the Continental money haint worth a sixpence a peck.

Crist. I think I'll re enlist in the army then, and be a soljer all my life, I feel so proud of the profession, there's so much glory in it. You see, we fought for glory, marched for glory, starved for glory, got discharged full of glory, and turned out on the world for glory, and faith the Continental Congress will let us poor divils die for glory, for all they care. Be gorry, they'll have to keep me if I enlist, unless they give me a trading post on the frontier—

Krout. (Slapping him on the shoulder and taking him aside.) Say, look here, 1 got a goot friend in Congress, what can get you dat job. Just give me $1,000 00 for expenses, and I'll make you a little acquainted with him. Believe me. *(Hand on breast.)* It was all right,—1 don't was squeelen. You bet!

Crist. Does your friend sell them jobs?

Krout. Oh, yaw; he makes out pooty goot, too, now.

Crist. Have ye one for yourself, or phat are ye going to do?

Krout. (To all.) Say, what you dink. So soon as das enemy gone oud from New York, I go in and buy out a lager beer saloon, and go in business right away mitt my-self. I'll sell Limburger, hand case, pretzels, herrings and all dat kind of business, und when you come by my house, don't you forgot your old friend, Lieutenant Jacob Krout, what fighted, bleet and died a couple of dimes by the side of George Washington.

Seth. Well, now that's kinder sensible Lieutenant, but where on earth are you going to get enough money to start business in? It will take a shipload of this inflated currency to buy a keg of lager beer.

Krout. I never thought me of dat. Let me see—

Crist. Faith, I knowed you hadn't a penny since you lost all you had playing Sex and-Sextig.

Krout. Lat me see,—where I get me the money—

Samp. I declar, Massa Jake, dat's a puzzler,—High!

Seth. Out with it, Lieutenant, like the father said to his boy, when he swallowed an acre of gingerbread.

Krout. I kan't dink me now.—lat's see—I was just like all Dutchmans, poor. Too proud to beg, and, by tam, too honest too steal. *(Pause.)* Oh, I got him now.

Seth. Well, where you going to make the raise?

Krout. I got him! I was too proud to beg, too honest to steal; and so I do like all Americaner big bugs, I bor-row me a couple of hundred thousand thalers, von Credit Mobilier stock. Odder, I can make him an under Amer-

icaner way; I go find my old partner. I got the experience of the business and he got the capital. In a couple
of years I got the capital mit the business, and he got
some experience. Ver, stayh! Well, Captain, what was
you going to do, anyhow?

Seth. Don't exactly know,—going back to Boston,
that's certain. Reckon I can get some governm-nt office
Get a fat contract to make head stones for the graves of
soldiers killed and died during the war. There's millions
in it!

Samp Take care now, Captain, when you get dat job,
don't go for to sticking up tomb-stones over mule bones
and call 'em dead soljers. I've heard of dat afore,—dat's
a dam insult to we soljers who fought and died in the
war. I's gwine to do a heap of good in my day. I's
gwine with General Washington to Mount Vernon down
on the old Potomac, and in a hundred years from now
you'll hear tell of dat nigger who took care of Massa
Washington in his old days. He took care of me when
I come nigh kicking the bucket in Valley Forge, and he
and Doctor Lincoln saved me wid a little rum and 'lasses

Seth Well, boys, our passes are up, we must go to
camp, and before we leave for home we will call on Buell.
(*Exit R*)

CHANGE.

SCENE III —*Same as Scene I. Two large flower vases
on table. ROSE and KATE discovered in wedding costumes of period 1776, attended by their maids arranging head-dresses*

Kate Rose, the Doctor informed me that General Washington is in the city, and being told that the Major is
stopping here temporarily, there is a possibility of the
General's calling to day.

Rose. I venture to say, that both the Doctor and the
Major extended him an invitation to be present at our
weddings.

Kate. Possibly, but our lords should not practice such
artful surprises on us so soon. Oh, I doubt very much
as to being honored by a call from him.

Rose. The presence of that dear face, the Preserver of
our Country, would be as memorable an epoch in our his
tory, as this, our wedding day

Kate. Why, so it would. Who would have thought
that I too would be led to the Altar of Hymen with you?
But inscrutable are the ways of Divine Providence.

Rose. The Doctor, no doubt, thought of it The merry
twinkling of his eye spoke plainer than words. He was
confident when he was beseiging you—using your military
phrase—that you would capitulate and surrender uncon-
ditionally about the time your sister would. (*Bell rings,
without.*)

Kate. (*Looking out of window.*) Why, here are the
bridegrooms. (*To* MAID) Sarah, please step to the door
and show them into the sitting-room. (MAID *going to
C. D.*)

Rose. And excuse us for a few moments, too. (*Exit*
MAID.)

Kate. The carriages are at the door.

Rose. Has the Major's nephew arrived with them?

Kate. No, they come unaccompanied in their own carriage.

Rose. I hope nothing will detain his nephew, or we
would be in a pretty plight; no relation of any of the con-
tracting parties would be present to give the brides away.

(*Re-enter* MAID *with bouquets.*)

Maid (*Giving bouquet to* ROSE.) The Major's compliments (*Giving bouquet to* KATE.) The Doctor's compliments.

Rose and Kate. Thanks.

Kate. Sarah, please help me with my veil.

Rose. And I am ready for mine. (*They arrange veils.*)
There, now, you may show them in. (*Exit* MAID.)

(ROSE *and* KATE *view themselves in glasses.*)

(*Enter* BUELL *and* DOCTOR. ROSE *meets* BUELL, *and* KATE
the DOCTOR. *they shake extended hands of the Bridegrooms with both of theirs.*)

Kate. (*To* BUELL.) Good morrow, Major.

Rose. (*To* DOCTOR) Good morrow, Doctor.

Buell. Good morrow, Miss Kate.

Doc. Good morrow, Miss Rose.

(*Rose and Buell go to Settee R., and Kate and Doctor to Settee L.,*)

Doc. Ladies, we hope to find you in a perfect state of salubrity, this morning. Haven't seen you look so charm—

Rose Tut, tut, Doctor! The old compliment. This is no time to listen to little words of useless flattery, just reserve them for the future.

Buell. Reserve them for whom, for you?

Rose Oh, no.

Doc Why, Major, I hope you are not getting jealous of your brother-in-law, so soon?

Kate. Of course not, Doctor. He accords you the same rights he takes Why, he has been talking love to me for weeks—

Doc For weeks?

Buell. Don't get jealous, Doctor.

Kate. That was before I met you though. *(All laugh.)*

Doc. Oh, was it? Well, I'll not get jealous. You are about to become my wife, and to think of getting jealous at this moment would blight my future happiness, cool my devotion, and destroy that confidence due all faithful lovers.

Kate. Ha, ha, ha! Doctor, you are getting in a fit of poetry.

Buell (At settee) My dear Rose, this day I claim those long coveted jewels I prize so dearly, your heart and hand.

Rose. In exchange, I claim my love's faithful vow for mine.—*(Enter Servant C D.)* Well, sir?

Servant. Captain Seth Peabody, and some friends of Major Buell and Doctor Lincoln.

Kate. Friends of the Doctors, why certainly admit them
(Exit Servant,—Church bells ringing)

Buell. The church bells ringing and my nephew not here, what can that mean?

Rose. Colonel Pomeroy may yet arrive in time. Probably something delays him a few moments.

(*Enter Seth, Krout, Crist, Sampson at C. D., Sampson turns back*)

Buell. Don't get scared Sampson, come in. (SAMPSON *comes back*)

Seth Why, how-do you-do-Major? (*Shaking hands.*)

Buell Very well, thank you, Captain. (CRIST *shakes hands with* DOCTOR) Ladies, Captain Seth Peabody; Lieutenant Jacob Krout; Sergeant Crist O'Rieley, and, Sampson Foster, of Ole Wirginny. (*They all courtesy*)

Rose and Kate. Welcome to you all, gentlemen.

Kate. Old companions in arms, I presume?

Samp. Jes' so, Misses, Jes' so.

Seth (*Aside to* BUELL) I say, Major, what's all this going on here?

Crist. (*Aside to* DOCTOR) Doctor, phat's all this fine fixing on the ladies mean?

(KROUT *and* SAMPSON *talk apart.*)

Buell. Gentlemen, you call at a happy time, and an explanation is necessary: The Doctor and myself—and I am sure our betrothed wives too—will feel much honored by your presence at our double wedding to-day.

Krout. I dought me it was someding like das. Well, I don't care, I stay mit you.

Crist. Faith, that we will.

Seth. Hang me, if I don't stay a week before I go home to Bosting to show Mrs. Peabody her husband, and after seven years' absence at that.

(*Enter* SERVANT *with letter for* BUELL *and returns.*)

Buell. This is from the Colonel. (*Opens and reads.*) "DEAR UNCLE BUELL:—I much regret that I must forego the honor of being present at your wedding The Hudson River was so swollen that I could not cross the ferry with my carriage in time to reach you. Will arrive by evening. A pleasant time to you and yours.

Your nephew,

COL. ALLEN POMEROY.

This will necessitate the selection of one to act in his stead. Who do you propose?

(*Enter* SERVANT.)

Servant. General Washington.

Omnes. General Washington.

(*Enter* WASHINGTON.)

Wash. Pray pardon my intrusion, ladies and gentle
men.

Doc. (*Approaching him*) A most welcome intruder.
General, (*Presenting him to* KATE.) the future Lady Lin
coln.   (KATE *courtesies.*)

Buell. (*Presenting* ROSE) General, allow me to pre
sent to you the future Lady Pomeroy.   The wedding
ceremony takes place this morning, and nothing would
give us more joy than to be honored with your presence.

Wash. Your wish shall be gratified.   I assure you,
gentlemen, nothing will give me more joy than to see such
faithful officers united to the choice of their hearts.   La
dies, accept my congratulations in your choice of worldly
protectors; braver and more valiant gentlemen are not to
be found.

Rose and Kate. Thanks, General, thanks.

Rose. General, everything is prepared and the wedding
bells are ringing, but just at this moment intelligence
reached us, that the only living relation of the contract
ing parties is unable to be present to officiate in giving
the brides away, therefore, I venture to say that the Fath
er of our Country will not deny us the honor to officiate
in his stead.

Wash. I only feel too much honored to comply with
your request, ladies.

Buell. The General, then, will lead as usual.   (*Wash
ington offers his arm to the ladies. Exits C. D.*)   Gen
tlemen, will you escort us to the Chapel ?

Seth. Excuse us, Major, we will stay here and welcome
you back.

Buell. Then help yourselves to refreshments in the
sideboard there. (*Exit* MAIDS *with* BUELL *and* DOCTOR.)

Samp. Golly, dat's de Major out and out, and, dog
gone me, if his gal ain't the verry pusson that done give
me dat bucket of flowers on that are march a couple weeks
ago.

Crist. And the other one is the same dear creature that
put that wreath around my neck.   I only wished it were
them arms of hers at the time.

Krout. (*Going to wing.*) Whar de duyfel ish dat side
board mit der refreshments.

Seth Ring the bell, Squire, that's the way we call for things at hum (*Sitting with feet up on table.*)

Krout. (*Strikes bell on table*) Wo bist dere, come arouse! (*Enter* SERVANT *from L. U. E.*) Pring in dat sideboard. putty guick!

Seth. Never mind the sideboard. fetch in the refresh ments. (*Exit* SERVANT.)

Samp Golly, we's gwine to hab some re-fresh er-ments.

Krout. Say, Sashant, don't they got a little limburger here, too?

Crist. What de divil d'ye want limburgur for, do ye want to stink the house out? What do ye want to be eating for every day? Did ye not have something to eat day-before-yesterday? What. do ye want to make a glutton of yourself?

(*Enter* SERVANT *with tray, wine bottles and glasses.*)

Krout. (*Taking bottle.*)Yaw, yaw, dat's de stuff, Rhine wine.

Seth. Fill 'em up for us, Lieutenant, and get your hand in for business. (*He fills up and they all drink.*)

Crist Let's have another; fill 'em up again.

Krout. (*Disgustingly.*) What, Sashant, do you want to make a glutton von yourself? (*Drinks out of bottle.*)

Crist. (*Taking bottle from him*) Hould on, Dutchey, just don't he making one of yourself.

Seth. Krout, now give us a song.

Omnes. Song! Song!

Krout. I got a cold, but I'll try. (*Sings a song.*)

Omnes. Good, good!

Crist. Well, boys, lets fill 'em up and drink to the health of the fair ladies and gentlemen, just gone to the church. (*Drink again.*) Be Gorry, they are back already.

(*Exit* SERVANT *with tray, glasses, &c, L. U. E.*)

(*Enter* BUELL *and* ROSE *and go to R.* WASHINGTON *down on A* DOCTOR *and* KATE *go to L.* MAIDS *enter and assist the brides at toilet. Lively Music.*)

Seth Ladies and gentlemen, I congratulate you all for myself and the rest of us. May you all have a long life, and a happy one.

All. Same to you, gentlemen. (*All courtesy.*)

Samp. (*Aside to* CRIST *and* KROUT.) Doesn't we all kiss the brides?

Crist. Hould your gob, ye ondacint beast, who de div'l would kiss you?

Samp. Why, they all does it in Ole Wirginny.
(BUELL *strikes bell on table.*)

Buell. Gentlemen, let us take a little wine before dinner. (*Enter* SERVANT *L. U. E.*, *and* BUELL *crosses, whispers.* *Exit* SERVANT. *Door-bell rings.*)

Rose. A call at the door. Answer it, Sarah. (*Exit* MAID *at* C. D. *Enter* SERVANT *L. U. E*, *with wine and fills glasses.*)

Buell. (*Passing wine around.*) General, you will find that to be an excellent quality.

Wash. (*Rising.*) Ladies and gentlemen, a pleasant journey through life. (*All rise.*)

Krout. Und ladies and shentlemen, I give you the old Pennsylvania toast: "Here's to your health and your families—"

Crist. (*Nudging him.*) They have no family.

rout. (*Aside to* CRIST.) Youst wait a little. "Und may you long live und prosper." (*All drink.*)
(*Enter* MAID *followed by four* CONGRESSMEN.)

Maid. Gentlemen, to see General Washington.

1st Cong. Intruding on a wedding party? (*Offers to retire.*)

Buell. Not in the least, sir; remain, gentlemen.

2d Cong. Our humble congratulations then to the happy parties.

Doc. Take a little wine with us, gentlemen. (*Fills and carries wine around.* WASHINGTON *shakes hands with* CONG., *and introduces them.*)

3d Cong. (*To* BUELL.) We come to tender Washington the nomination for the Presidency.

Buell. Then let it be tendered to him here.

4th Cong. Our best wishes, ladies and gentlemen. (*All raise glasses.*)

Buell. And, long live George Washington, the Father of our Country, and First President of the United States.
(*All drink but* WASH.)

Rose. You are not drinking, General.

Wash. Not to the latter, but to the first with pleasure.
Omnes. Drink to both!   (WASH. *drinks.*)
Omnes. (*Cheers.*)
1st *Cong.* (*To* BUELL) With your permission we will
make known our busines to General Washington here.
               (BUELL *bows in acquiescence.*)
1st *Cong.* General, the impossibility to govern the
country by a Congress since the close of the war, grew
every day more and more apparent, and consequently the
recent convention, of which you were the honored presi
dent, gave us the Constitution of the United States, and
the first step for us to take provided by that constitution
will be the election of a President.   All eyes are turned
to you; and we are appointed by your fellow countrymen
to tender you the nomination.   (OMNES *cheers*)
Wash. Fellow countrymen, I must decline in accord-
ance with my firm resolution, made known to you through
my farewell address to the army, from accepting any public office. I hoped then to become a private citizen on
the banks of the Potomac; and, under the shadow of my
own vine and fig tree, free from the bustle of a camp and
busy scene of public life, to solace myself with those tran-
quil enjoyments of which the soldier and statesman have
but little conception.
1st *Cong.* General, break your resolve for once. To
see the goodly fabric you have reared with so much toil
and care fall to the ground, and the nation you have saved
from bondage become the by-word and scoff of Kings, is
a contemplation from which we turn our faces. We appeal, sir, to your love and devotion to your country, and
we call on you to rescue it once more.
Wash. (*After a pause.*) You use an unkind weapon,
and apply it unrelentingly on the only weak point I possess,—love of country. I, reluctantly, accept the nomination.
2d *Cong.* And a grateful country will acknowledge that
debt of gratitude and love due to its defender and most
honored citizen, by placing him in the highest office within the gift of a free, brave and liberty-loving people. He,
whose arm wielded the invincible sword of victory, and
pointed out to us a Free Country, will establish justice,

insure domestic tranquility. promote the general welfare, and secure the blessings of liberty to ourselves and our posterity for centuries to come. Long live Washington!

Omnes. Long live Washington! (*Prolonged cheers.*)

DISPOSITION OF CHARACTERS.

MAID   MAID.

SETH.   SAMP.   KROUT. CRIST.

BUELL AND ROSE.   DOCTOR AND KATE.

CONGRESSMEN.   WASHINGTON   CONGRESSMEN.

Quick Curtain.

CURTAIN RISES ON TABLEAU—"WASHINGTON RESIGNS HIS

SWORD TO CONGRESS."